DUO

DUO

Marcia Muller
and
Bill Pronzini

Five Star
Unity, Maine

Five Star Mystery.
Published in conjunction with Tekno-Books and Ed Gorman.

Cover photograph by Jason Johnson.

November 1998
Standard Print Hardcover Edition.

Five Star Standard Print Mystery Series.

The text of this edition is unabridged.

Set in 11 pt. Plantin by Minnie B. Raven.

Printed in the United States on permanent paper.

Library of Congress Cataloging in Publication Data

Muller, Marcia.
    Duo : stories / by Marcia Muller and Bill Pronzini.
      p. cm.
    ISBN 0-7862-1657-3 (hc : alk. paper)
    1. Detective and mystery stories, American.
I. Pronzini, Bill. II. Title.
PS3563.U397D86   1998
  813´.54—dc21
                                                 98-42591

Acknowledgments:

Contents:

Part I:

Stories by
Marcia Muller

The Cracks in the Sidewalk

GRACIE

I'm leaning against my mailbox and the sun's shining on my face and my pigeons are coming round. Storage box number 27368. The mail carrier's already been here — new one, because he didn't know my name and kind of shied away from me like I smell bad. Which I probably do. I'll have him trained soon, though, and he'll say "Hi, Gracie" and pass the time of day and maybe bring me something to eat. Just the way the merchants in this block do. It's been four years now, and I've got them all trained. Box 27368 — it's gotten to be like home.

Home . . .

Nope, I can't think about that. Not anymore.

Funny how the neighborhood's changed since I started taking up space on this corner with my cart and my pigeons, on my blanket on good days, on plastic in the rain. Used to be the folks who lived in this part of San Francisco was Mexicans and the Irish ran the bars and used-furniture stores. Now you see a lot of Chinese or whatever, and there're all these new restaurants and coffeehouses. Pretty fancy stuff. But that's okay; they draw a nice class of people, and the waiters bring me the leftovers. And my pigeons are still the same — good company. They're sort of like family.

Family . . .

No, I can't think about that anymore.

CECILY

I've been watching the homeless woman they call Gracie for two years now, ever since I left my husband and moved into the studio over the Lucky Shamrock and started to write my novel. She shows up every morning promptly at nine and sits next to the mail-storage box and holds court with the pigeons. People in the neighborhood bring her food, and she always shares it with the birds. You'd expect them to flock all over her, but instead they hang back respectfully, each waiting its turn. It's as if Gracie and they speak the same language, although I've never heard her say a word to them.

How to describe her without relying on the obvious stereotypes of homeless persons? Not that she isn't stereotypical: She's ragged and she smells bad and her gray-brown hair is long and tangled. But in spite of the wrinkles and roughness of her skin, she seems ageless, and on days like this when she smiles and turns her face up to the sun she has a strange kind of beauty. Beauty disrupted by what I take to be flashes of pain. Not physical, but psychic pain — the reason, perhaps, that she took up residence on the cracked sidewalk of the Mission District.

I wish I knew more about her.

All I know are these few things: She's somewhere in her late thirties, a few years older than I. She told the corner grocer that. She has what she calls a "hidey-hole" where she goes to sleep at night — someplace safe, she told the mailman, where she won't be disturbed. She guards her shopping cart full of plastic bags very carefully; she'd kill anyone who touched it, she warned my landlord. She's been coming here nearly four years and hasn't missed a single day; Deirdre, the bartender at the Lucky Shamrock, has kept track. She was born in Oroville, up in the foothills of the Sierras; she mentioned that to my neighbor when she saw him

12

wearing a sweatshirt saying OROVILLE — BEST LITTLE CITY BY A DAM SITE.

And that's it.

Maybe there's a way to find out more about her. Amateur detective work. Call it research, if I feel a need to justify it. Gracie might make a good character for a story. Anyway, it would be something to fool around with while I watch the mailbox and listen for the phone, hoping somebody's going to buy my damn novel. Something to keep my mind off this endless cycle of hope and rejection. Something to keep my mind off my regrets.

Yes, maybe I'll try to find out more about Gracie.

GRACIE

Today I'm studying on the cracks in the sidewalk. They're pretty complicated, running this way and that, and on the surface they look dark and empty. But if you got down real close and put your eye to them there's no telling what you might see. In a way the cracks're like people. Or music.

Music . . .

Nope, that's something else I can't think about.

Seems the list of what I can't think on is getting longer and longer. Bits of the past tug at me, and then I've got to push them away. Like soft summer nights when it finally cools and the lawn sprinklers twirl on the grass. Like the sleepy eyes of a little boy when you tuck him into bed. Like the feel of a guitar in your hands.

My hands.

My little boy.

Soft summer nights up in Oroville.

No.

Forget the cracks, Gracie. There's that woman again —

13

the one with the curly red hair and green eyes that're always watching. Watching *you*. Talking about you to the folks in the stores and the restaurants. Wonder what she wants?

Not my cart — it better not be my cart. My gold's in there.

My gold . . .

No. That's at the top of the list.

CECILY

By now I've spoken with everybody in the neighborhood who's had any contact with Gracie, and only added a few details to what I already know. She hasn't been back to Oroville for over ten years, and she never will go back; somebody there did a "terrible thing" to her. When she told that to my neighbor, she became extremely agitated and made him a little afraid. He thought she might be about to tip over into a violent psychotic episode, but the next time he saw her she was as gentle as ever. Frankly, I think he's making too much of her rage. He ought to see the heap of glass I had to sweep off my kitchenette floor yesterday when yet another publisher returned my manuscript.

Gracie's also quite familiar with the Los Angeles area — she demonstrated that in several random remarks she made to Deirdre. She told at least three people that she came to San Francisco because the climate is mild and she knew she'd have to live on the street. She sings to the pigeons sometimes, very low, and stops right away when she realizes somebody's listening. My landlord's heard her a dozen times or more, and he says she's got a good voice. Oh, yes — she doesn't drink or do drugs. She told one of the waiters at Gino's that she has to keep her mind clear so she can control it — whatever that means.

Not much to go on. I wish I could get a full name for

her; I'm not even sure Gracie *is* her name. God, I'm glad to have this little project to keep me occupied! Disappointments pile on disappointments lately, and sometimes I feel as if I were trapped in one of those cracks in the sidewalk that obviously fascinate Gracie. As if I'm being squeezed tighter and tighter . . .

Enough of that. I think I'll go to the library and see if they have that book on finding people that I heard about. Technically, Gracie isn't lost, but her identity's missing. Maybe the book would give me an idea of how to go about locating it.

GRACIE

Not feeling so good today, I don't know why, and that red-haired woman's snooping around again. Who the hell is she? A fan?

Yeah, sure. A fan of old Gracie. Old Gracie, who smells bad and has got the look of a loser written all over her.

House of cards, he used to say. It can all collapse at any minute, and then how'll you feel about your sacrifices? *Sacrifices.* The way he said it, it sounded like a filthy word. But I never gave up anything that mattered. Well, one thing, one person — but I didn't know I was giving him up at the time.

No, no, *no!*

The past's tugging at me more and more, and I don't seem able to push it away so easy. Control, Gracie. But I'm nor feeling good, and I think it's gonna rain. Another night in my hidey-hole with the rain beating down, trying not to remember the good times. The high times. The times when —

No.

CECILY

What a joke my life is. Three thanks-but-no-thanks letters from agents I'd hoped would represent me, and I can't even get the Gracie project off the ground. The book I checked out of the library was about as helpful — as my father used to say — as tits on a billygoat. Not that it wasn't informative and thorough. Gracie's just not a good subject for that kind of investigation.

I tried using the data sheet in the appendix. Space at the top for name: Gracie. Also known as: ? Last known address: Oroville, California — but that was more than ten years ago. Last known phone number: ? Automobiles owned, police record, birth date, Social Security number, real estate owned, driver's license number, profession, children, relatives, spouse: all blank. Height: five feet six, give or take. Weight: too damn thin. Present location: divides time between postal storage box 27368 and hidey-hole, location unknown.

Some detective, me.

Give it up, Cecily. Give it up and get on with your life. Take yourself downtown to the temp agency and sign on for a three-month job before your cash all flows out. Better yet, get yourself a real, permanent job and give up your stupid dreams. They aren't going to happen.

But they might. Wasn't I always one of the lucky ones? Besides, they tell you that all it takes is one editor who likes your work. They tell you all it takes is keeping at it. A page a day, and in a year you'll have a novel. One more submission, and soon you'll see your name on a book jacket. And there's always the next manuscript. This Gracie would make one hell of a character, might even make the basis for a good novel. If only I could find out . . .

The cart. Bet there's something in that damned cart that

16

she guards so carefully. Tomorrow I think I'll try to be-
friend Gracie.

GRACIE

Feeling real bad today, even my pigeons sense it and leave me
alone. That red-haired woman's been sneaking around. This
morning she brought me a bagel slathered in cream cheese
just the way I like them. I left the bagel for the pigeons, fed the
cream cheese to a stray cat. I know a bribe when I see one.

Bribes. There were plenty: a new car if you're a good girl.
A new house, too, if you cooperate. And there was the biggest bribe of all, the one they never came through with. . . .

No.

Funny, things keep misting over today, and I'm not even
crying. Haven't cried for years. No, this reminds me more of
the smoky neon haze and the flashing lights. The sea of
faces that I couldn't pick a single individual out of. Smoky
sea of faces, but it didn't matter. The one I wanted to see
wasn't there.

Bribes, yeah. Lies, really. *We'll make sure everything's
worked out. Trust us. It's taking longer than we thought. He's
making it difficult. Be patient. And by the way, we're not too
sure about this new material.*

Bribes . . .

The wall between me and the things on my list of what
not to remember is crumbling. Where's my control? That
wall's my last defense. . . .

CECILY

Deirdre's worried about Gracie. She's looking worse than
usual and has been refusing food. She fed the bagel I brought

17

her to the pigeons, even though Del at Gino's said bagels with cream cheese are one of her favorite things. Deirdre thinks we should do something — but what?

Notify her family? Not possible. Take her to a hospital? She's not likely to have health insurance. I suppose there's always a free clinic, but would she agree to go? I doubt it. There's no doubt she's shutting out the world, though. She barely acknowledges anyone.

I think I'll follow her to her hidey-hole tonight. We ought to know where it is, in case she gets seriously ill. Besides, maybe there's a clue to who she is secreted there.

GRACIE

The pigeons've deserted me, guess they know I'm not really with them anymore. I'm mostly back there in the smoky neon past and the memories're really pulling hard now. The unsuspecting look on my little boy's face and the regret in my heart when I tucked him in, knowing it was the last time. The rage on his father's face when I said I was leaving. The lean times that weren't really so lean because I sure wasn't living like I am today. The high times that didn't last. The painful times when I realized they weren't going to keep their promises.

It'll be all right. We'll arrange everything.

But it wasn't all right and nothing got arranged. It'll never be all right again.

CECILY

Gracie's hidey-hole is an abandoned trash Dumpster behind a condemned building on 18th Street. I had quite a time finding it. The woman acts like a criminal who's afraid she's being tailed, and it took three nights of ducking into doorways and

18

hiding behind parked cars to follow her there. I watched through a hole in the fence while she unloaded the plastic bags from her cart to the Dumpster, then climbed in after them. The clang when she pulled the lid down was deafening, and I can imagine how noisy it is in there when it rains, like it's starting to right now. Anyway, Gracie's home for the night.

Tomorrow morning after she leaves I'm going to investigate that Dumpster.

GRACIE

Rain thundering down hard, loud and echoing like applause. It's the only applause old Gracie's likely to hear anymore.

Old Gracie, that's how I think of myself. And I'm only thirty-nine, barely middle-aged. But I crammed a lot into those last seventeen years, and life catches up with some of us faster than others. I don't know as I'd have the nerve to look in a mirror anymore. What I'd see might scare me.

That red-haired woman was following me for a couple of nights — after my gold, for sure — but today I didn't see her. How she knows about the gold, I don't know. I never told anybody, but that must be it, it's all I've got of value. I'm gonna have to watch out for her, but keeping on guard is one hell of a job when you're feeling like I do.

It must be the rain. If only this rain'd stop, I'd feel better.

CECILY

Checking out that Dumpster was about the most disgusting piece of work I've done in years. It smelled horrible, and the stench is still with me — in my hair and on my clothing. The bottom half is covered with construction debris like two-by-fours and Sheetrock, and on top of it Gracie's made a nest of unbelievably filthy bedding. At first I thought there wasn't anything of hers there and, frankly, I wasn't too enthusiastic about searching thoroughly. But then, in a space between some planking beneath the wad of bedding, I found a cardboard gift box — heart-shaped and printed with roses that had faded almost to white. Inside it were some pictures of a little boy.

He was a chubby little blond, all dressed up to have his photo taken, and on the back of each somebody had written his name — Michael Joseph — and the date. In one he wore a party hat and had his hand stuck in a birthday cake, and on its back was the date — March 8, 1975 — and his age — two years.

Gracie's little boy? Probably. Why else would she have saved his pictures and the lock of hair in the blue envelope that was the only other thing in the box?

So now I have a lead. A woman named Gracie (if that's her real name) had a son named Michael Joseph on March 8, 1973, perhaps in Oroville. Is that enough information to justify a trip up to Butte County to check the birth records? A trip in my car, which by all rights shouldn't make it to the San Francisco county line?

Well, why not? I collected yet another rejection letter yesterday. I need to get away from here.

GRACIE

I could tell right away when I got back tonight — somebody's been in my hidey-hole. Nothing looked different, but I could smell whoever it was, the way one animal can smell another.

I guess that's what it all boils down to in the end: We're not much different from the animals.

I'll stay here tonight because it's raining again and I'm

weary from the walk and unloading my cart. But tomorrow I'm out of here. Can't stay where it isn't safe. Can't sleep in a place somebody's defiled.

Well, they didn't find anything. Everything I own was in my cart. Everything except the box with the pictures of Mikey. They disappeared a few years ago, right about the time I moved in here. Must've fallen out of the cart, or else somebody took them. Doesn't matter, though; I remember him as clear as if I'd tucked him in for the last time only yesterday. Remember his father, too, cursing me as I went out the door, telling me I'd never see my son again.

I never did.

I remember all the promises, too; my lawyer and my manager were going to work it all out so I could have Mikey with me. But his father made it difficult and then things went downhill and then there was the drug bust and all the publicity —

Why am I letting the past suck me in? All those years I had such good control. No more drink, no more drugs, just pure, strong control. A dozen years on the street, first down south, then up here, and I always kept my mind on the present and its tiny details. My pigeons, the people passing by, the cracks in the sidewalk . . .

It's like I've tumbled into one of those cracks. I'm falling and I don't know what'll happen next.

CECILY

Here I am in Oroville, in a cheap motel not far from the Butte County Courthouse. By all rights I shouldn't have made it this far. The car tried to die three times — once while I was trying to navigate the freeway maze at Sacramento — but I arrived before the vital statistics department

21

closed. And now I know who Gracie is!

Michael Joseph Venema was born on March 8, 1973, to Michael William and Grace Ann Venema in Butte Hospital. The father was thirty-five at the time, the mother only sixteen. Venema's not a common name here; the current directory lists only one — initial *M* — on Lark Lane. I've already located it on the map, and I'm going there tomorrow morning. It's a Saturday, so somebody's bound to be at home. I'll just show up and maybe the element of surprise will help me pry loose the story of my neighborhood bag lady.

God, I'm good at this! Maybe I should scrap my literary ambitions and become an investigative reporter.

GRACIE

I miss my Dumpster. Was noisy when it rained, that's true, but at least it was dry. The only shelter I could find tonight was this doorway behind Gino's, and I had to wait for them to close up before I crawled into it, so I got plenty wet. My blankets're soaked, but the plastic has to go over my cart to protect my things. How much longer till morning?

Well, how would I know? Haven't had a watch for years. I pawned it early on, that was when I was still sleeping in hotel rooms, thinking things would turn around for me. Then I was sleeping in my car and had to sell everything else, one by one. And then it was a really cheap hotel, and I turned some tricks to keep the money coming, but when a pimp tried to move in on me, I knew it was time to get my act together and leave town. So I came here and made do. In all the years I've lived on the street in different parts of this city, I've never turned another trick and I've never panhandled. For a while before I started feeling so bad I picked up little jobs, working just for food. But lately I've had to rely on other people's kindnesses.

It hurts to be so dependent.

There's another gust of wind, blowing the rain at me. It's raining like a son of a bitch tonight. It better let up in the morning.

I miss my Dumpster. I miss . . .

No. I've still got *some* control left. Not much, but a shred.

CECILY

Now I know Gracie's story, and I'm so distracted that I got on the wrong freeway coming back through Sacramento. There's a possibility I may be able to reunite her with her son Mike — plus I've got my novel, all of it, and it's going to be terrific! I wouldn't be surprised if it changed my life.

I went to Mike's house this morning — a little prefab on a couple of acres in the country south of town. He was there, as were his wife and baby son. At first he didn't believe his mother was alive, then he didn't want to talk about her. But when I told him Gracie's circumstances he opened up and agreed to tell me what he knew. And he knew practically everything, because his father finally told him the truth when he was dying last year.

Gracie was a singer. One of those bluesy-pop kind like Linda Ronstadt, whom you can't categorize as either country or Top 40. She got her start singing at their church and received some encouragement from a friend's uncle who was a sound engineer at an L.A. recording studio. At sixteen she'd married Mike's father — who was nearly twenty years her senior — and they'd never been very happy. So on the strength of that slim encouragement, she left him and their son and went to L.A. to try to break into the business.

And she did, under the name Grace Ventura. The interesting thing is, I remember her first hit, "Smoky Neon Haze," very clearly. It was romantic and tragic, and I was just at the age when tragedy is an appealing concept rather than a harsh reality.

Anyway, Mike's father was very bitter about Gracie deserting them — the way my husband was when I told him I was leaving to become a writer. After Gracie's first album did well and her second earned her a gold record, she decided she wanted custody of Mike, but there was no way his father would give him up. Her lawyer initiated a custody suit, but while that was going on Gracie's third album flopped. Gracie started drinking and doing drugs and couldn't come up with the material for a fourth album; then she was busted for possession of cocaine, and Mike's father used that against her to gain permanent custody. And then the record company dropped her. She tried to make a comeback for a couple of years, then finally disappeared. She had no money; she'd signed a contract that gave most of her earnings to the record label, and what they didn't take, her manager and lawyer did. No wonder she ended up on the streets.

I'm not sure how Mike feels about being reunited with his mother; he was very noncommittal. He has his own life now, and his printing business is just getting off the ground. But he did say he'd try to help her, and that's the message I'm to deliver to Gracie when I get back to the city.

I hope it works out. For Gracie's sake, of course, and also because it would make a perfect upbeat ending to my novel.

24

GRACIE

It's dry and warm here in the storage room. Deirdre found me crouched behind the garbage cans in the alley a while ago and brought me inside. Gave me some blankets she borrowed from one of the folks upstairs. They're the first clean things I've had next to my skin in years.

Tomorrow she wants to take me to the free clinic. I won't go, but I'm grateful for the offer.

Warm and dry and dark in here. I keep drifting — out of the present, into the past, back and forth. No control now. In spite of the dark I can see the lights — bright colors, made hazy by the smoke. Just like in that first song . . . what was it called? Don't remember. Doesn't matter.

It was a good one, though. Top of the charts. Didn't even surprise me. I always thought I was one of the lucky ones.

I can see the faces, too. Seems like acres of them, looking up at me while I'm blinded by the lights. Listen to the applause! For me. And that didn't surprise me, either. I always knew it would happen. But where was that? When?

Can't remember. Doesn't matter.

Was only one face that ever mattered. Little boy. Who was he?

Michael Joseph. Mikey.

Funny, for years I've fought the memories. Pushed them away when they tugged, kept my mind on the here and now. Then I fell into the crack in the sidewalk, and it damn near swallowed me up. Now the memories're fading, except for one. Michael Joseph. Mikey.

That's a good one. I'll hold on to it.

CECILY

Gracie died last night in the storeroom at the Lucky Shamrock. Deirdre brought her in there to keep her out of the rain, and when she looked in on her after closing, she was dead. The coroner's people said it was pneumonia; she'd probably been walking around with it for a long time, and the soaking finished her.

I cried when Deirdre told me. I haven't cried in years, and there I was, sobbing over a woman whose full name I didn't even know until two days ago.

I wonder why she wasn't in her hidey-hole. Was it because she realized I violated it and didn't feel safe anymore? God, I hope not! But how could she have known?

I wish I could've told her about her son, that he said he'd help her. But maybe it's for the best, after all. Gracie might have wanted more than Mike was willing to give her — emotionally, I mean. Besides, she must've been quite unbalanced toward the end.

I guess it's for the best, but I still wish I could've told her.

This morning Deirdre and I decided we'd better go through the stuff in her cart, in case there was anything salvageable that Mike might want. Some of the plastic bags were filled with ragged clothing, others with faded and crumbling clippings that chronicled the brief career of Grace Ventura. There was a Bible, some spangled stage costumes, a few paperbacks, a bundle of letters about the custody suit, a set of keys to a Mercedes, and other mementos that were in such bad shape we couldn't tell what they'd been. But at the very bottom of the cart, wrapped in rags and more plastic bags, was the gold record awarded to her for her second album, "Soft Summer Nights."

On one hand, not much to say for a life that once held

such promise. On the other hand, it says it all.

It gives me pause. Makes me wonder about my own life. Is all of this worth it? I really don't know. But I'm not giving up — not now, when I've got Gracie's story to tell. I wouldn't be the least bit surprised if it changed my life.

After all, aren't I one of the lucky ones?

Aren't I?

Sweet Cactus Wine

The rain stopped as suddenly as it had begun, the way it always does in the Arizona desert. The torrent had burst from a near-cloudless sky, and now it was clear once more, the land nourished. I stood in the doorway of my house, watching the sun touch the stone wall, the old buckboard and the twisted arms of the giant saguaro cacti.

The suddenness of these downpours fascinated me, even though I'd lived in the desert for close to forty years, since the day I'd come here as Joe's bride in 1866. They'd been good years, not exactly bountiful, but we'd lived here in quiet comfort. Joe had the instinct that helped him bring the crops — melons, corn, beans — from the parched soil, an instinct he shared with the Papago Indians who were our neighbors. I didn't possess the knack, so now that he was gone I didn't farm. I did share one gift with the Papagos, however — the ability to make sweet cactus wine from the fruit of the saguaro. That wine was my livelihood now — as well as, I must admit, a source of Saturday-night pleasure — and the giant cacti scattered around the ranch were my fortune.

I went inside to the big rough-hewn table where I'd been shelling peas when the downpour started. The bowl sat there half full, and I eyed the peas with distaste. Funny what age will do to you. For years I'd had an overly hearty appetite. Joe used to say, "Don't worry, Katy. I like big women." Lucky for him he did, because I'd carried around enough lard for two such admirers, and I didn't believe in

28

divorce anyway. Joe'd be surprised if he could see me now, though. I was tall, yes, still tall. But thin. I guess you'd call it gaunt. Food didn't interest me any more.

I sat down and finished shelling the peas anyway. It was market day in Arroyo, and Hank Gardner, my neighbor five miles down the road, had taken to stopping in for supper on his way home from town. Hank was widowed too. Maybe it was his way of courting. I didn't know and didn't care. One man had been enough trouble for me and, anyway, I intended to live out my days on these parched but familiar acres.

Sure enough, right about suppertime Hank rode up on his old bay. He was a lean man, browned and weathered by the sun like folks get in these parts, and he rode stiffly. I watched him dismount, then went and got the whiskey bottle and poured him a tumblerful. If I knew Hank, he'd had a few drinks in town and would be wanting another. And a glassful sure wouldn't be enough for old Hogsbreath Hank, as he was sometimes called.

He came in and sat at the table like he always did. I stirred the iron pot on the stove and sat down too. Hank was a man of few words, like my Joe had been. I'd heard tales that his drinking and temper had pushed his wife into an early grave. Sara Gardner had died of pneumonia, though, and no man's temper ever gave that to you.

Tonight Hank seemed different, jumpy. He drummed his fingers on the table and drank his whiskey.

To put him at his ease, I said, "How're things in town?"

"What?"

"Town. How was it?"

"Same as ever."

"You sure?"

"Yeah, I'm sure. Why do you ask?" But he looked kind of furtive.

"No reason," I said. "Nothing changes out here. I don't know why I asked." Then I went to dish up the stew. I set it and some corn bread on the table, poured more whiskey for Hank and a little cactus wine for me. Hank ate steadily and silently. I sort of picked at my food.

After supper I washed up the dishes and joined Hank on the front porch. He still seemed jumpy, but this time I didn't try to find out why. I just sat there beside him, watching the sun spread its redness over the mountains in the distance. When Hank spoke, I'd almost forgotten he was there.

"Kathryn" — he never called me Katy; only Joe used that name — "Kathryn, I've been thinking. It's time the two of us got married."

So that was why he had the jitters. I turned to stare. "What put an idea like that into your head?"

He frowned. "It's natural."

"Natural?"

"Kathryn, we're both alone. It's foolish you living here and me living over there when our ranches sit next to each other. Since Joe went, you haven't farmed the place. We could live at my house, let this one go, and I'd farm the land for you."

Did he want me or the ranch? I know passion is supposed to die when you're in your sixties, and as far as Hank was concerned mine had, but for form's sake he could at least pretend to some.

"Hank," I said firmly, "I've got no intention of marrying again — or of farming this place."

"I said I'd farm it for you."

"If I wanted it farmed, I could hire someone to do it. I wouldn't need to acquire another husband."

"We'd be company for one another."

"We're company now."

"What're you going to do — sit here the rest of your days scratching out a living with your cactus wine?"

"That's exactly what I plan to do."

"Kathryn . . ."

"No."

"But . . ."

"No. That's all."

Hank's jaw tightened and his eyes narrowed. I was afraid for a minute that I was going to be treated to a display of his legendary temper, but soon he looked placid as ever. He stood, patting my shoulder.

"You think about it," he said. "I'll be back tomorrow and I want a yes answer."

I'd think about it, all right. As a matter of fact, as he rode off on the bay I was thinking it was the strangest marriage proposal I'd ever heard of. And there was no way old Hogsbreath was getting any yesses from me.

He rode up again the next evening. I was out gathering cactus fruit. In the springtime, when the desert nights are still cool, the tips of the saguaro branches are covered with waxy white flowers. They're prettiest in the hours around dawn, and by the time the sun hits its peak, they close. When they die, the purple fruit begins to grow, and now, by midsummer, it was splitting open to show its bright red pulp. That pulp was what I turned into wine.

I stood by my pride and joy — a fifty-foot giant that was probably two hundred years old — and watched Hank come toward me. From his easy gait, I knew he was sure I'd changed my mind about his proposal. Probably figured he was irresistible, the old goat. He had a surprise coming.

"Well, Kathryn," he said, stopping and folding his arms

across his chest, "I'm here for my answer."

"It's the same as it was last night. No. I don't intend to marry again."

"You're a foolish woman, Kathryn."

"That may be. But at least I'm foolish in my own way."

"What does that mean?"

"If I'm making a mistake, it'll be one I decide on, not one you decide for me."

The planes of his face hardened, and the wrinkles around his eyes deepened. "We'll see about that." He turned and strode toward the bay.

I was surprised he had backed down so easy, but relieved. At least he was going.

Hank didn't get on the horse, however. He fumbled at his saddle scabbard and drew his shotgun. I set down the basket of cactus fruit. Surely he didn't intend to shoot me!

He turned, shotgun in one hand.

"Don't be a fool, Hank Gardner."

He marched toward me. I got ready to run, but he kept going, past me. I whirled, watching. Hank went up to a nearby saguaro, a twenty-five footer. He looked at it, turned and walked exactly ten paces. Then he turned again, brought up the shotgun, sighted on the cactus, and began to fire. He fired at its base over and over.

I put my hand to my mouth, shutting off a scream.

Hank fired again, and the cactus toppled.

It didn't fall like a man would if he were shot. It just leaned backwards. Then it gave a sort of sigh and leaned farther and farther. As it leaned it picked up momentum, and when it hit the ground there was an awful thud.

Hank gave the cactus a satisfied nod and marched back toward his horse.

I found my voice. "Hey, you! Just what do you think you're doing?"

Hank got on the bay. "Cactuses are like people, Kathryn. They can't do anything for you once they're dead. Think about it."

"You bet I'll think about it! That cactus was valuable to me. You're going to pay!"

"What happens when there're no cactuses left?"

"What? What?"

"How're you going to scratch out a living on this miserable ranch if someone shoots all your cactuses?"

"You wouldn't dare!"

He smirked at me. "You know, there's one way cactuses *aren't* like people. Nobody ever hung a man for shooting one."

Then he rode off.

I stood there speechless. Did the bastard plan to shoot up my cacti until I agreed to marry him?

I went over to the saguaro. It lay on its back, oozing water. I nudged it gently with my foot. There were a few round holes in it — entrances to the caves where the Gila woodpeckers lived. From the silence, I guessed the birds hadn't been inside when the cactus toppled. They'd be mighty surprised when they came back and found their home on the ground.

The woodpeckers were the least of my problems, however. They'd just take up residence in one of the other giants. Trouble was, what if Hank carried out his veiled threat? Then the woodpeckers would run out of nesting places — and I'd run out of fruit to make my wine from.

I went back to the granddaddy of my cacti and picked up the basket. On the porch I set it down and myself in my rocking chair to think. What was I going to do?

I could go to the sheriff in Arroyo, but the idea didn't please me. For one thing, like Hank had said, there was no law against shooting a cactus. And for another, it was embarrassing to be in this kind of predicament at my age. I could see all the locals lined up at the bar of the saloon, laughing at me. No, I didn't want to go to Sheriff Daly if I could help it.

So what else? I could shoot Hank, I supposed, but that was even less appealing. Not that he didn't deserve shooting, but they could hang you for murdering a man, unlike a cactus. And then, while I had a couple of Joe's old rifles, I'd never been comfortable with them, never really mastered the art of sighting and pulling the trigger. With my luck, I'd miss Hank and kill off yet another cactus.

I sat on the porch for a long time, puzzling and listening to the night sounds of the desert. Finally I gave up and went to bed, hoping the old fool would come to his senses in the morning.

He didn't, though. Shotgun blasts on the far side of the ranch brought me flying out of the house the next night. By the time I got over there, there was nothing around except a couple of dead cacti. The next night it happened again, and still the next night. The bastard was being cagey, too. I had no way of proving it actually was Hank doing the shooting. Finally I gave up and decided I had no choice but to see Sheriff Daly.

I put on my good dress, fixed my hair and hitched up my horse to the old buckboard. The trip into Arroyo was hot and dusty, and my stomach lurched at every bump in the road. It's no fun knowing you're about to become a laughingstock. Even if the sheriff sympathized with me, you can bet he and the boys would have a good chuckle afterwards.

I drove up Main Street and left the rig at the livery stable. The horse needed shoeing anyway. Then I went down the wooden sidewalk to the sheriff's office. Naturally, it was closed. The sign said he'd be back at two, and it was only noon now. I got out my list of errands and set off for the feed store, glancing over at the saloon on my way.

Hank was coming out of the saloon. I ducked into the shadow of the covered walkway in front of the bank and watched him, hate rising inside me. He stopped on the sidewalk and waited, and a moment later a stranger joined him. The stranger wore a frock coat and a broad-brimmed black hat. He didn't dress like anyone from these parts. Hank and the man walked toward the old adobe hotel and shook hands in front of it. Then Hank ambled over to where the bay was tied, and the stranger went inside.

I stood there, frowning. Normally I wouldn't have been curious about Hank Gardner's private business, but when a man's shooting up your cacti you develop an interest in anything he does. I waited until he had ridden off down the street, then crossed and went into the hotel.

Sonny, the clerk, was a friend from way back. His mother and I had run church bazaars together for years, back when I still had the energy for that sort of thing. I went up to him and we exchanged pleasantries.

Then I said, "Sonny, I've got a question for you, and I'd just as soon you didn't mention me asking it to anybody."

He nodded.

"A man came in here a few minutes ago. Frock coat, black hat."

"Sure. Mr. Johnson."

"Who is he?"

"You don't know?"

"I don't get into town much these days."

"I guess not. Everybody's talking about him. Mr. Johnson's a land developer. Here from Phoenix."

Land developer. I began to smell a rat. A rat named Hank Gardner.

"What's he doing, buying up the town?"

"Not the town. The countryside. He's making offers on all the ranches." Sonny eyed me thoughtfully. "Maybe you better talk to him. You've got a fair-sized spread there. You could make good money. In fact, I'm surprised he hasn't been out to see you."

"So am I, Sonny. So am I. You see him, you tell him I'd like to talk to him."

"He's in his room now. I could . . ."

"No." I held up my hand. "I've got a lot of errands to do. I'll talk to him later."

But I didn't do any errands. Instead I went home to sit in my rocker and think.

That night I didn't light my kerosene lamp. I kept the house dark and waited at the front door. When the evening shadows had fallen, I heard a rustling sound. A tall figure slipped around the stone wall into the dooryard.

I watched as he approached one of the giant saguaros in the dooryard. He went right up to it, like he had the first one he'd shot, turned and walked exactly ten paces, then blasted away. The cactus toppled, and Hank ran from the yard.

I waited. Let him think I wasn't to home. After about fifteen minutes, I got undressed and went to bed in the dark, but I didn't rest much. My mind was too busy planning what I had to do.

The next morning I hitched up the buckboard and drove over to Hank's ranch. He was around back, mending a harness. He started when he saw me. Probably figured I'd come to shoot him. I got down from the buckboard and walked up to him, a sad, defeated look on my face.

"You're too clever for me, Hank. I should have known it."

"You ready to stop your foolishness and marry me?"

"Hank," I lied, "there's something more to my refusal than just stubbornness."

He frowned. "Oh?"

"Yes. You see, I promised Joe on his deathbed that I'd never marry again. That promise means something to me."

"I don't believe in . . ."

"Hush. I've been thinking, though, about what you said about farming my ranch. I've got an idea. Why *don't* you farm it for me? I'll move in over here, keep house and feed you. We're old enough everyone would know there weren't any shenanigans going on."

Hank looked thoughtful, pleased even. I'd guessed right; it wasn't my fair body he was after.

"That might work. But what if one of us died? Then what?"

"I don't see what you mean."

"Well, if you died, I'd be left with nothing to show for all that farming. And if I died, my son might come back from Tucson and throw you off the place. Where would you be then?"

"I see." I looked undecided, fingering a pleat in my skirt. "That *is* a problem." I paused. "Say, I think there's a way around it."

"Yeah?"

"Yes. We'll make wills. I'll leave you my ranch in mine. You do the same in yours. That way we'd both have something to show for our efforts."

He nodded, looking foxy. "That's a good idea, Kathryn.

Very good." I could tell he was pleased I'd thought of it myself.

"And, Hank, I think we should do it right away. Let's go into town this afternoon and have the wills drawn up."

"Fine with me." He looked even more pleased. "Just let me finish with this harness."

The will signing, of course, was a real solemn occasion. I even sniffed a little into my handkerchief before I put my signature to the document. The lawyer, Will Jones, was a little surprised by our bequests, but not much. He knew I was alone in the world, and Hank's son John was known to be more of a ne'er-do-well than his father. Probably Will Jones was glad to see the ranch wouldn't be going to John.

I had Hank leave me off at my place on his way home. I wanted, I said, to cook him one last supper in my old house before moving to his in the morning. I went about my preparations, humming to myself. Would Hank be able to resist rushing back into town to talk to Johnson, the land developer? Or would he wait a decent interval, say a day?

Hank rode up around sundown. I met him on the porch, twisting my handkerchief in my hands.

"Kathryn, what's wrong?"

"Hank, I can't do it."

"Can't do what?"

"I can't leave the place. I can't leave Joe's memory. This whole thing's been a terrible mistake."

He scowled. "Don't be foolish. What's for supper?"

"There isn't any."

"What?"

"How could I fix supper with a terrible mistake like this on my mind?"

"Well, you just get in there and fix it. And stop talking this way."

I shook my head. "No, Hank, I mean it. I can't move to your place. I can't let you farm mine. It wouldn't be right. I want you to go now, and tomorrow I'm going into town to rip up my will."

"You what?" His eyes narrowed.

"You heard me, Hank."

He whirled and went toward his horse. "You'll never learn, will you?"

"What are you going to do?"

"What do you think? Once your damned cactuses are gone, you'll see the light. Once you can't make any more of that wine, you'll be only too glad to pack your bags and come with me."

"Hank, don't you dare!"

"I do dare. There won't be a one of them standing."

"Please, Hank! At least leave my granddaddy cactus." I waved at the fifty-foot giant in the outer dooryard. "It's my favorite. It's like a child to me."

Hank grinned evilly. He took the shotgun from the saddle and walked right up to the cactus.

"Say good-bye to your child."

"Hank! Stop!"

He shouldered the shotgun.

"Say good-bye to it, you foolish woman."

"Hank, don't you pull that trigger!"

He pulled it.

Hank blasted at the giant saguaro — one, two, three times. And, like the others, it began to lean.

Unlike the others, though, it didn't lean backwards. It gave a great sigh and leaned and leaned and leaned forwards. And then it toppled. As it toppled, it picked up momentum. And when it fell on Hank Gardner, it made an awful thud.

I stood quietly on the porch. Hank didn't move. Finally I went over to him. Dead. Dead as all the cacti he'd murdered.

I contemplated his broken body a bit before I hitched up the buckboard and went to tell Sheriff Daly about the terrible accident. Sure was funny, I'd say, how that cactus toppled forwards instead of backwards. Almost as if the base had been partly cut through and braced so it would do exactly that.

Of course, the shotgun blasts would have destroyed any traces of the cutting.

Cattails

We came around the lake, Frances and I, heading toward the picnic ground. I was lugging the basket and when the going got rough, like where the path narrowed to a ledge of rock, I would set it down a minute before braving the uneven ground.

All the while I was seeing us as if we were in a movie — something I do more and more the older I get.

They come around the lake, an old couple of seventy, on a picnic. The woman strides ahead, still slender and active, her red scarf fluttering in the breeze. He follows, carrying the wicker basket, a stooped gray-headed man who moves hesitantly, as if he is a little afraid.

Drama, I thought. We're more and more prone to it as the real thing fades from our lives. We make ourselves stars in scenarios that are at best boring. Ah, well, it's a way to keep going. I have my little dramas; Frances has her spiritualism and séances. And, thinking of keeping going, I must or Frances will tell me I'm good for nothing, not even carrying the basket to the picnic ground.

Frances had already arrived there by the time I reached the meadow. I set the basket down once more and mopped my damp brow. She motioned impatiently to me and, with a muttered "Yes, dear," I went on. It was the same place we always came for our annual outing. The same sunlight glinted coldly on the water; the same chill wind blew up from the shore; the same dampness saturated the ground.

January. A hell of a time for a picnic, even here in the

hills of Northern California. I knew why she insisted on it. Who would know better than I? And yet I wondered — was there more to it than that? Was the fool woman trying to kill me with these damned outings?

She spread the plaid blanket on the ground in front of the log we always used as a backrest. I lowered myself onto it, groaning. Yes, the ground was damp as ever. Soon it would seep through the blanket and into my clothes. Frances unpacked the big wicker basket, portioning out food like she did at home. It was a nice basket, with real plates and silverware, all held in their own little niches. Frances had even packed cloth napkins — leave it to her not to forget. The basket was the kind you saw advertised nowadays in catalogs for rich people to buy, but it hadn't cost us very much. I'd made the niches myself and outfitted it with what was left of our first set of dishes and flatware. That was back in the days when I liked doing handy projects, before . . .

"Charles, you're not eating." Frances thrust my plate into my hands.

Ham sandwich. On rye. With mustard. Pickle, garlic dill. Potato salad, Frances's special recipe. The same as always.

"Don't you think next year we could have something different?" I asked.

Frances looked at me with an expression close to hatred. "You know we can't."

"Guess not." I bit into the sandwich.

Frances opened a beer for me. Bud. I'm not supposed to drink, not since the last seizure, and I've been good, damned good. But on these yearly picnics it's different. It's got to be.

Frances poured herself some wine. We ate in silence, staring at the cattails along the shore of the lake.

When we finished what was on our plates, Frances opened another beer for me and took out the birthday cake.

It was chocolate with darker chocolate icing. I knew that without looking.

"He would have been twenty-nine," she said.

"Yes."

"Twenty-nine. A man."

"Yes," I said again, with mental reservations.

"Poor Richie. He was such a beautiful baby."

I was silent, watching the cattails.

"Do you remember, Charles? What a beautiful baby he was?"

"Yes."

That had been in Detroit. Back when the auto industry was going great guns and jobs on the assembly line were a dime a dozen. We'd had a red-brick house in a suburb called Royal Oak. And a green Ford — that's where I'd worked, Ford's, the River Rouge plant — and a yard with big maple trees. And, unexpectedly, we'd had Richie.

"He was such a good baby, too. He never cried."

"No, he didn't."

Richie never cried. He'd been unusually silent, watching us. And I'd started to drink more. I'd come home and see them, mother and the change-of-life baby she'd never wanted, beneath the big maple trees. And I'd go to the kitchen for a beer.

I lost the job at Ford's. Our furniture was sold. The house went on the market. And then we headed west in the green car. To Chicago.

Now Frances handed me another beer.

"I shouldn't." I wasn't used to drinking anymore and I already felt drunk.

"Drink it."

I shrugged and tilted the can.

Chicago had been miserable. There we'd lived in a rail-

43

road flat in an old dark brick building. It was always cold in the flat, and in the Polish butcher shop where I clerked. Frances started talking about going to work, but I wouldn't let her. Richie needed her. Needed watching.

The beer was making me feel sleepy.

In Chicago, the snow had drifted and covered the front stoop. I would come home in the dark, carrying meat that the butcher shop was going to throw out — chicken backs and nearly spoiled pork and sometimes a soupbone. I'd take them to the kitchen, passing through the front room where Richie's playpen was, and set them on the drainboard. And then I'd go to the pantry for a shot or two of something to warm me. It was winter when the green Ford died. It was winter when I lost the job at the butcher shop. A snowstorm was howling in off Lake Michigan when we got on the Greyhound for Texas. I'd heard of work in Midland.

Beside me, Frances leaned back against the log. I set my empty beer can down and lay on my side.

"That's right, Charles, go to sleep." Her voice shook with controlled anger, as always.

I closed my eyes, traveling back to Texas.

Roughnecking the oil rigs hadn't been easy. It was hard work, dirty work, and for a newcomer, the midnight shift was the only one available. But times hadn't been any better for Frances and Richie. In the winter, the northers blew through every crack in the little box of a house we'd rented. And summer's heat turned the place into an oven. Frances never complained. Richie did, but, then, Richie complained about everything.

Summer nights in Midland were the only good times. We'd sit outside, sometimes alone, sometimes with neighbors, drinking beer and talking. Once in a while we'd go to a roadhouse, if we could find someone to take care of Richie.

That wasn't often, though. It was hard to find someone to stay with such a difficult child. And then I fell off the oil rig and broke my leg. When it healed, we boarded another bus, this time for New Mexico.

I jerked suddenly. Must have dozed off. Frances sat beside me, clutching some cattails she'd picked from the edge of the lake while I slept. She set them down and took out the blue candles and started sticking them on the birthday cake.

"Do you remember that birthday of Richie's in New Mexico?" She began lighting the candles, all twenty-nine of them.

"Yes."

"We gave him that red plastic music box? Like an organ grinder's? With the fuzzy monkey on top that went up and down when you turned the handle?"

"Yes." I looked away from the candles to the cattails and the lake beyond. The monkey had gone up and down when you turned the handle — until Richie had stomped on the toy and smashed it to bits.

In Roswell we'd had a small stucco house, nicer than the one in Midland. Our garden had been westernized — that's what they call pebbles instead of grass, cacti instead of shrubs. Not that I spent a lot of time there. I worked long hours in the clothing mill.

Frances picked up the cattails and began pulling them apart, scattering their fuzzy insides. The breeze blew most of the fluff away across the meadow, but some stuck to the icing on the cake.

"He loved that monkey, didn't he?"

"Yes," I lied.

"And the tune the music box played — what was it?"

" 'Pop Goes the Weasel.' " But she knew that.

"Of course. 'Pop Goes the Weasel.' " The fuzz continued to drift through her fingers. The wind from the lake blew some of it against my nose. It tickled.

"Roswell was where I met Linda," Frances added. "Do you remember her?"

"There's nothing wrong with my memory."

"She foretold it all."

"Some of it."

"All."

I let her have the last word. Frances was a stubborn woman.

Linda. Roswell was where Frances had gotten interested in spiritualism, foretelling the future, that sort of stuff. I hadn't liked it, but, hell, it gave Frances something to do. And there was little enough to do, stuck out there in the desert. I had to hand it to Linda — she foretold my losing the job at the clothing mill. And our next move, to Los Angeles.

Frances was almost done with the cattails. Soon she'd ask me to get her some more.

Los Angeles. A haze always hanging over the city. Tall palms that were nothing but poles with sickly wisps of leaves at the top. And for me, job after job, each worse, until I was clerking at the Orange Julius for minimum wage. For Frances and Richie it wasn't so bad, though. We lived in Santa Monica, near the beach. Nothing fancy, but she could take him there and he'd play in the surf. It kept him out of trouble — he'd taken to stealing candy and little objects from the stores. When they went to the beach on weekends I stayed home and drank.

"I need some more cattails, Charles."

"Soon."

Was the Orange Julius the last job in L.A.? Funny how

46

they all blended together. But it had to be — I was fired from there after Richie lifted twenty dollars from the cash register while visiting me. By then we'd scraped together enough money from Frances's baby-sitting wages to buy an old car — a white Nash Rambler. It took us all the way to San Francisco and these East Bay hills where we were sitting today.

"Charles, the cattails."

"Soon."

The wind was blowing off the lake. The cattails at the shore moved, beckoning me. The cake was covered with white fuzz. The candles guttered, dripping blue wax.

"Linda," Frances said. "Do you remember when she came to stay with us in Oakland?"

"Yes."

"We had the séance."

"Yes."

I didn't believe in the damned things, but I'd gone along with it. Linda had set up chairs around the dining-room table in our little shingled house. The room had been too small for the number of people there and Linda had made cutting remarks. That hurt. It was all we could afford. I was on disability then because of the accident at the chemical plant. I'd been worrying about Richie's adjustment problems in school and my inattention on the job had caused an explosion.

"That was my first experience with those who have gone beyond," Frances said now.

"Yes."

"You didn't like it."

"No, I didn't."

There had been rapping noises. And chill drafts. A dish had fallen off a shelf. Linda said afterward it had been a young spirit we had contacted. She claimed young spirits were easier to raise.

I still didn't believe in any of it. Not a damned bit!

"Charles, the cattails."

I stood up.

Linda had promised to return to Oakland the next summer. We would all conduct more "fun" experiments. By the time she did, Frances was an expert in those experiments. She'd gone to every charlatan in town after that day in January, here at the lake. She'd gone because on that unseasonably warm day, during his birthday picnic at this very meadow, Richie had drowned while fetching cattails from the shore. Died by drowning, just as Linda had prophesied in New Mexico. Some said it had been my fault because I'd been drunk and had fallen asleep and failed to watch him. Frances seemed to think so. But Frances had been wandering around in the woods or somewhere and hadn't watched him either.

I started down toward the lake. The wind had come up and the overripe cattails were breaking open, their white fuzz trailing like fog.

Funny. They had never done that before.

I looked back at Frances. She motioned impatiently.

I continued down to the lakeside.

Frances had gone to the mediums for years, hoping to make contact with Richie's spirit. When that hadn't worked, she went less and spiritualism became merely a hobby for her. But one thing she still insisted on was coming here every year to reenact the fatal picnic. Even though it was usually cold in January, even though others would have stayed away from the place where their child had died, she came and went through the ritual. Why? Anger at me, I supposed. Anger because I'd been drunk and asleep that day . . .

The cattail fuzz was thicker now. I stopped. The lake was obscured by it. Turning, I realized I could barely see Frances.

Shapes seemed to be forming in the mist.

The shape of Richie. A bad child.

The shape of Frances. An unhappy mother.

"Daddy, help!"

The cry seemed to come out of the mist at the water's edge. I froze for a moment, then started down there. The mist got thicker. Confused, I stopped. Had I heard something? Or was it only in my head?

Drama, I thought. Drama . . .

The old man stands enveloped in the swirling mist, shaking his gray head. Gradually his sight returns. He peers around, searching for the shapes. He cocks his head, listening for another cry. There is no sound, but the shapes emerge. . . .

A shape picking cattails. And then another, coming through the mist, arm outstretched. Then pushing. Then holding the other shape down. Doing the thing the old man has always suspected but refused to accept.

The mist began to settle. I turned, looked back up the slope. Frances was there, coming at me. Her mouth was set; I hadn't returned with the cattails.

Don't come down here, Frances, I thought. It's dangerous down here now that I've seen those shapes and the mist has cleared. Don't come down.

Frances came on toward me. She was going to bawl me out for not bringing the cattails. I waited.

One of these days, I thought, it might happen. Maybe not this year, maybe not next, but someday it might. Someday I might drown *you*, Frances, just as — maybe — you drowned our poor, unloved son Richie that day so long ago. . . .

Somewhere in the City

(A Sharon McCone Story)

At 5:04 P.M. on October 17, 1989, the city of San Francisco was jolted by an earthquake that measured a frightening 7.1 on the Richter Scale. The violent tremors left the Bay Bridge impassable, collapsed a double-decker freeway in nearby Oakland, and toppled or severely damaged countless homes and other buildings. From the Bay Area to the seaside town of Santa Cruz some 100 miles south, 65 people were killed and thousands left homeless. And when the aftershocks subsided, San Francisco entered a new era — one in which things would never be quite the same. As with all cataclysmic events, the question "where were you when?" will forever provoke deeply emotional responses in those of us who lived through it. . . .

WHERE I WAS WHEN: the headquarters of the Golden Gate Crisis Hotline in the Noe Valley district. I'd been working a case there — off and on, and mostly in the late afternoon and evening hours, for over two weeks — with very few results and with a good deal of frustration.

The hotline occupied one big windowless room behind a rundown coffeehouse on Twenty-fourth Street. The location, I'd been told, was not so much one of choice as of convenience (meaning the rent was affordable), but had I not known that, I would have considered it a stroke of genius. There was something instantly soothing about entering through the coffeehouse, where the aromas of various blends permeated the air and steam rose from huge stainless-steel urns. The patrons were unthreatening — mostly shabby and relaxed, reading or conversing with their feet propped up on chairs. The pastries displayed in the glass case were comfort food at its purest — reminders of the days when calories and cholesterol didn't count. And the round face of the proprietor, Lloyd Warner, was welcoming and kind as he waved troubled visitors through to the crisis center.

On that Tuesday afternoon I arrived at about twenty to five, answering Lloyd's cheerful greeting and trying to ignore the chocolate-covered doughnuts in the case. I had a dinner date at seven-thirty, had been promised some of the best French cuisine on Russian Hill, and was unwilling to spoil my appetite. The doughnuts called out to me, but I turned a deaf ear and hurried past.

The room beyond the coffeehouse contained an assortment of mismatched furniture: several desks and chairs of all vintages and materials; phones in colors and styles ranging from standard black touchtone to a shocking turquoise princess; three tattered easy chairs dating back to the fifties; and a card table covered with literature on health and psychological services. Two people manned the desks nearest the door. I went to the desk with the turquoise phone, plunked my briefcase and bag down on it, and turned to face them.

"He call today?" I asked.

Pete Lowry, a slender man with a bandit's mustache who

was director of the center, took his booted feet off the desk and swiveled to face me. "Nope. It's been quiet all afternoon."

"Too quiet." This came from Ann Potter, a woman with dark frizzed hair who affected the aging-hippie look in jeans and flamboyant over-blouses. "And this weather — I don't like it one bit."

"Ann's having one of her premonitions of gloom and doom," Pete said. "Evil portents and omens lurk all around us — although most of them went up front for coffee a while ago."

Ann's eyes narrowed to a glare. She possessed very little sense of humor, whereas Pete perhaps possessed too much. To forestall the inevitable spat, I interrupted. "Well, I don't like the weather much myself. It's muggy and too warm for October. It makes me nervous."

"Why?" Pete asked.

I shrugged. "I don't know, but I've felt edgy all day."

The phone on his desk rang. He reached for the receiver. "Golden Gate Crisis Hotline, Pete speaking."

Ann cast one final glare at his back as she crossed to the desk that had been assigned to me. "It has been too quiet," she said defensively. "Hardly anyone's called, not even to inquire about how to deal with a friend or a family member. That's not normal, even for a Tuesday."

"Maybe all the crazies are out enjoying the warm weather."

Ann half-smiled, cocking her head. She wasn't sure if what I'd said was funny or not, and didn't know how to react. After a few seconds her attention was drawn to the file I was removing from my briefcase. "Is that about our problem caller?"

"Uh-huh." I sat down and began rereading my notes silently, hoping she'd go away. I'd meant it when I'd said I felt on edge, and was in no mood for conversation.

The file concerned a series of calls that the hotline had received over the past month — all from the same individual, a man with a distinctive raspy voice. Their content had been more or less the same: an initial plaint of being all alone in the world with no one to care if he lived or died; then a gradual escalating from despair to anger, in spite of the trained counselors' skillful responses; and finally the declaration that he had an assault rifle and was going to kill others and himself. He always ended with some variant on the statement, "I'm going to take a whole lot of people with me."

After three of the calls, Pete had decided to notify the police. A trace was placed on the center's lines, but the results were unsatisfactory; most of the time the caller didn't stay on the phone long enough, and in the instances that the calls could be traced, they turned out to have originated from booths in the Marina district. Finally, the trace was taken off, the official conclusion being that the calls were the work of a crank — and possibly one with a grudge against someone connected with the hotline.

The official conclusion did not satisfy Pete, however. By the next morning he was in the office of the hotline's attorney at All Souls Legal Cooperative, where I am chief investigator. And a half an hour after that, I was assigned to work the phones at the hotline as often as my other duties permitted, until I'd identified the caller. Following a crash course from Pete in techniques for dealing with callers in crisis — augmented by some reading of my own — they turned me loose on the turquoise phone.

After the first couple of rocky, sweaty-palmed sessions,

I'd gotten into it: become able to distinguish the truly disturbed from the fakers or the merely curious; learned to gauge the responses that would work best with a given individual; succeeded at eliciting information that would permit a crisis team to go out and assess the seriousness of the situation in person. In most cases, the team would merely talk the caller into getting counseling. However, if they felt immediate action was warranted, they would contact the SFPD, who had the authority to have the individual held for evaluation at S.F. General Hospital for up to seventy-two hours.

During the past two weeks the problem caller had been routed to me several times, and with each conversation I became more concerned about him. While his threats were melodramatic, I sensed genuine disturbance and desperation in his voice; the swift escalation of panic and anger seemed much out of proportion to whatever verbal stimuli I offered. And, as Pete had stressed in my orientation, no matter how theatrical or frequently made, any threat of suicide or violence toward others was to be taken with the utmost seriousness by the hotline volunteers.

Unfortunately I was able to glean very little information from the man. Whenever I tried to get him to reveal concrete facts about himself, he became sly and would dodge my questions. Still, I could make several assumptions about him: he was youngish, reasonably well-educated, and Caucasian. The traces to the Marina indicated he probably lived in that bayside district — which meant he had to have a good income. He listened to classical music (three times I'd heard it playing in the background) from a transistor radio, by the tinny tonal quality. Once I'd caught the call letters of the FM station — one with a wide-range signal in the Central Valley town of Fresno. Why Fresno? I'd wondered. Perhaps he was from there? But that wasn't much to go on; there were probably several Fresno transplants in his part of the city.

When I looked up from my folder, Ann had gone back to her desk. Pete was still talking in low, reassuring tones with his caller. Ann's phone rang, and she picked up the receiver. I tensed, knowing the next call would cycle automatically to my phone.

When it rang some minutes later, I glanced at my watch and jotted down the time while reaching over for the receiver. Four-fifty-eight. "Golden Gate Crisis Hotline, Sharon speaking."

The caller hung up — either a wrong number or, more likely, someone who lost his nerve. The phone rang again about twenty seconds later and I answered it in the same manner.

"Sharon. It's me." The greeting was the same as the previous times, the raspy voice unmistakable.

"Hey, how's it going?"

A long pause, labored breathing. In the background I could make out the strains of music — Brahms, I thought. "Not so good. I'm really down today."

"You want to talk about it?"

"There isn't much to say. Just more of the same. I took a walk a while ago, thought it might help. But the people, out there flying their kites, I can't take it."

"Why is that?"

"I used to . . . ah, forget it."

"No, I'm interested."

"Well, they're always in couples, you know."

When he didn't go on, I made an interrogatory sound.

"The whole damn world is in couples. Or families. Even

55

here inside my little cottage I can feel it. There are these apartment buildings on either side, and I can feel them pressing in on me, and I'm here all alone."

He was speaking rapidly now, his voice rising. But as his agitation increased, he'd unwittingly revealed something about his living situation. I made a note about the little cottage between the two apartment buildings.

"This place where the people were flying kites," I said, "do you go there often?"

"Sure — it's only two blocks away." A sudden note of sullenness now entered his voice — a part of the pattern he'd previously exhibited. "Why do you want to know about that?"

"Because . . . I'm sorry, I forgot your name."

No response.

"It would help if I knew what to call you."

"Look, bitch, I know what you're trying to do."

"Oh?"

"Yeah. You want to get a name, an address. Send the cops out. Next thing I'm chained to the wall at S.F. General. I've been that route before. But I know my rights now; I went down the street to the Legal Switchboard, and they told me . . ."

I was distracted from what he was saying by a tapping sound — the stack trays on the desk next to me bumped against the wall. I looked over there, frowning. What was causing that . . . ?

". . . gonna take the people next door with me . . ."

I looked back at the desk in front of me. The lamp was jiggling.

"What the hell?" the man on the phone exclaimed.

My swivel chair shifted. A coffee mug tipped and rolled across the desk and into my lap.

Pete said, "Jesus Christ, we're having an earthquake!"

". . . The ceiling's coming down!" The man's voice was panicked now.

"Get under a door frame!" I clutched the edge of the desk, ignoring my own advice.

I heard a crash from the other end of the line. The man screamed in pain. "Help me! Please help —" And then the line went dead.

For a second or so I merely sat there — longtime San Franciscan, frozen by my own disbelief. All around me formerly inanimate objects were in motion. Pete and Ann were scrambling for the archway that led to the door of the coffeehouse.

"Sharon, get under the desk!" she yelled at me.

And then the electricity cut out, leaving the windowless room in blackness. I dropped the dead receiver, slid off the chair, crawled into the kneehole of the desk. There was a cracking, a violent shifting, as if a giant hand had seized the building and twisted it. Tremors buckled the floor beneath me.

This is a bad one. Maybe the big one that they're always talking about.

The sound of something wrenching apart. Pellets of plaster rained down on the desk above me. Time had telescoped; it seemed as if the quake had been going on for many minutes, when in reality it could not have been more than ten or fifteen seconds.

Make it stop! Please make it stop!

And then, as if whatever powers-that-be had heard my unspoken plea, the shock waves diminished to shivers, and finally ebbed.

Blackness. Silence. Only bits of plaster bouncing off the desks and the floor.

"Ann?" I said. "Pete?" My voice sounded weak, tentative.

"Sharon?" It was Pete. "You okay?"

"Yes. You?"

"We're fine."

Slowly I began to back out of the kneehole. Something blocked it — the chair. I shoved it aside, and emerged. I couldn't see a thing, but I could feel fragments of plaster and other unidentified debris on the floor. Something cut into my palm; I winced.

"God, it's dark," Ann said. "I've got some matches in my purse. Can you —"

"No matches," I told her. "Who knows what shape the gas mains are in."

". . . Oh, right."

Pete said, "Wait, I'll open the door to the coffeehouse."

On hands and knees I began feeling my way toward the sound of their voices. I banged into one of the desks, overturned a wastebasket, then finally reached the opposite wall. As I stood there, Ann's cold hand reached out to guide me. Behind her I could hear Pete fumbling at the door.

I leaned against the wall. Ann was close beside me, her breathing erratic. Pete said, "Goddamned door's jammed." From behind it came voices of the people in the coffeehouse.

Now that the danger was over — at least until the first of the aftershocks — my body sagged against the wall, giving way to tremors of its own manufacture. My thoughts turned to the lover with whom I'd planned to have dinner: where had he been when the quake hit? And what about my cats, my house? My friends and my co-workers at All Souls? Other friends scattered throughout the Bay Area?

And what about a nameless, faceless man somewhere in

the city who had screamed for help before the phone went dead?

The door to the coffeehouse burst open, spilling weak light into the room. Lloyd Warner and several of his customers peered anxiously through it. I prodded Ann — who seemed to have lapsed into lethargy — toward them.

The coffeehouse was fairly dark, but late afternoon light showed beyond the plate-glass windows fronting on the street. It revealed a floor that was awash in spilled liquid and littered with broken crockery. Chairs were tipped over — whether by the quake or the patrons' haste to get to shelter I couldn't tell. About ten people milled about, talking noisily.

Ann and Pete joined them, but I moved forward to the window. Outside, Twenty-fourth Street looked much as usual, except for the lack of traffic and pedestrians. The buildings still stood, the sun still shone, the air drifting through the open door of the coffeehouse was still warm and muggy. In this part of the city, at least, life went on.

Lloyd's transistor radio had been playing the whole time — tuned to the station that was carrying the coverage of the third game of the Bay Area World Series, due to start at five-thirty. I moved closer, listening.

The sportscaster was saying, "Nobody here knows *what's* going on. The Giants have wandered over to the A's dugout. It looks like a softball game where somebody forgot to bring the ball."

Then the broadcast shifted abruptly to the station's studios. A newswoman was relaying telephone reports from the neighborhoods. I was relieved to hear that Bernal Heights, where All Souls is located, and my own small district near Glen Park were shaken up but for the most part undamaged. The broadcaster concluded by warning listeners not

59

to use their phones except in cases of emergency. Ann snorted and said, "Do as I say but not . . ."

Again the broadcast made an abrupt switch — to the station's traffic helicopter. "From where we are," the reporter said, "it looks as if part of the upper deck on the Oakland side of the Bay Bridge has collapsed onto the bottom deck. Cars are pointing every whichway, there may be some in the water. And on the approaches —" The transmission broke, then resumed after a number of static-filled seconds. "It looks as if the Cypress Structure on the Oakland approach to the bridge has also collapsed. Oh my God, there are cars and people —" This time the transmission broke for good.

It was very quiet in the coffeehouse. We all exchanged looks — fearful, horrified. This was an extremely bad one, if not the catastrophic one they'd been predicting for so long.

Lloyd was the first to speak. He said, "I'd better see if I can insulate the urns in some way, keep the coffee hot as long as possible. People'll need it tonight." He went behind the counter, and in a few seconds a couple of the customers followed.

The studio newscast resumed. ". . . fires burning out of control in the Marina district. We're receiving reports of collapsed buildings there, with people trapped inside . . ."

The Marina district. People trapped.

I thought again of the man who had cried out for help over the phone. Of my suspicion, more or less confirmed by today's conversation, that he lived in the Marina.

Behind the counter Lloyd and the customers were wrapping the urns in dishtowels. Here — and in other parts of the city, I was sure — people were already overcoming their shock, gearing up to assist in the relief effort. There was nothing I could do in my present surroundings, but . . .

I hurried to the back room and groped until I found my

purse on the floor beside the desk. As I picked it up, an aftershock hit — nothing like the original trembler, but strong enough to make me grab the chair for support. When it stopped, I went shakily out to my car.

Twenty-fourth Street was slowly coming to life. People bunched on the sidewalks, talking and gesturing. A man emerged from one of the shops, walked to the center of the street and surveyed the facade of his building. In the parking lot of nearby Bell Market, employees and customers gathered by the grocery carts. A man in a butcher's apron looked around, shrugged, and headed for a corner tavern. I got into my MG and took a city map from the side pocket.

The Marina area consists mainly of early twentieth-century stucco homes and apartment buildings built on fill on the shore of the bay — which meant the quake damage there would naturally be bad. The district extends roughly from the Fisherman's Wharf area to the Presidio — not large, but large enough, considering I had few clues as to where within its boundary my man lived. I spread out the map against the steering wheel and examined it.

The man had said he'd taken a walk that afternoon, to a place two blocks from his home where people were flying kites. That would be the Marina Green near the Yacht Harbor, famous for the elaborate and often fantastical kites flown there in fine weather. Two blocks placed the man's home somewhere on the far side of Northpoint Street.

I had one more clue: in his anger at me he'd let it slip that the Legal Switchboard was "down the street." The switchboard, a federally-funded assistance group, was headquartered in one of the piers at Fort Mason, at the east end of the Marina. While several streets in that vicinity ended at Fort Mason, I saw that only two — Beach and Northpoint

— were within two blocks of the Green as well.

Of course, I reminded myself, "down the street" and "two blocks," could have been generalizations or exaggerations. But it was somewhere to start. I set the map aside and turned the key in the ignition.

The trip across the city was hampered by near-gridlock traffic on some streets. All the stoplights were out; there were no police to direct the panicked motorists. Citizens helped out: I saw men in three-piece suits, women in heels and business attire, even a ragged man who looked to be straight out of one of the homeless shelters, all playing traffic cop. Sirens keened, emergency vehicles snaked from lane to lane. The car radio kept reporting further destruction; there was another aftershock, and then another, but I scarcely felt them because I was in motion.

As I inched along a major crosstown arterial, I asked myself why I was doing this foolhardy thing. The man was nothing to me, really — merely a voice on the phone, always self-pitying, and often antagonistic and potentially violent. I ought to be checking on my house and the folks at All Souls; if I wanted to help people, my efforts would have been better spent in my own neighborhood or Bernal Heights. But instead I was traveling to the most congested and dangerous part of the city in search of a man I'd never laid eyes on.

As I asked the question, I knew the answer. Over the past two weeks the man had told me about his deepest problems. I'd come to know him in spite of his self-protective secretiveness. And he'd become more to me than just the subject of an investigation; I'd begun to care whether he lived or died. Now we had shared a peculiarly intimate moment — that of being together, if only in voice, when the catastrophe that San Franciscans feared the most had struck. He had called for help; I had heard his terror and pain. A connection had been established that could not be broken.

After twenty minutes and little progress, I cut west and took a less-traveled residential street through Japantown and over the crest of Pacific Heights. From the top of the hill I could see and smell the smoke over the Marina; as I crossed the traffic-snarled intersection with Lombard, I could see the flames. I drove another block, then decided to leave the MG and continue on foot.

All around I could see signs of destruction now: a house was twisted at a tortuous angle, its front porch collapsed and crushing a car parked at the curb; on Beach Street an apartment building's upper story had slid into the street, clogging it with rubble; three bottom floors of another building were flattened, leaving only the top intact.

I stopped at a corner, breathing hard, nearly choking on the thickening smoke. The smell of gas from broken lines was vaguely nauseating — frightening, too, because of the potential for explosions. To my left the street was cordoned off; fire-department hoses played on the blazes — weakly, because of damaged water mains. People congregated everywhere, staring about with horror-struck eyes; they huddled together, clinging so one another; many were crying. Firefighters and police were telling people to go home before dark fell. "You should be looking after your property," I heard one say. "You can count on going seventy-two hours without water or power."

"Longer than that," someone said.

"It's not safe here," the policeman added. "Please go home."

Between sobs, a woman said, "What if you've got no home to go to any more?"

The cop had no answer for her.

Emotions were flying out of control among the onlookers. It would have been easy to feed into it — to weep, even panic. Instead, I turned my back to the flaming buildings, began walking the other way, toward Fort Mason. If the man's home was beyond the barricades, there was nothing I could do for him. But if it lay in the other direction, where there was a lighter concentration of rescue workers, then my assistance might save his life.

I forced myself to walk slower, to study the buildings on either side of the street. I had one last clue that could lead me to the man: he'd said he lived in a little cottage between two apartment buildings. The homes in this district were mostly of substantial size; there couldn't be too many cottages situated in just that way.

Across the street a house slumped over to one side, its roof canted at a forty-five-degree angle, windows from an apartment house had popped out of their frames, and its iron fire escapes were tangled and twisted like a cat's cradle of yarn. Another home was unrecognizable, merely a heap of rubble. And over there, two four-story apartment buildings leaned together, forming an arch over a much smaller structure. . . .

I rushed across the street, pushed through a knot of bystanders. The smaller building was a tumble-down mass of white stucco with a smashed red tile roof and a partially flattened iron fence. It had been a Mediterranean-style cottage with grillwork over high windows; now the grills were bent and pushed outward; the collapsed windows resembled swollen-shut eyes.

The woman standing next to me was cradling a terrified cat under her loose cardigan sweater. I asked, "Did the man who lives in the cottage get out okay?"

She frowned, tightened her grip on the cat as it burrowed

deeper. "I don't know who lives there. It's always kind of deserted-looking."

A man in front of her said, "I've seen lights, but never anybody coming or going."

I moved closer. The cottage was deep in the shadows of the leaning buildings, eerily silent. From above came a groaning sound, and then a piece of wood sheared off the apartment house to the right, crashing onto what remained of the cottage's roof. I looked up, wondering how long before one or the other of the buildings toppled. Wondering if the man was still alive inside the compacted mass of stucco. . . .

A man in jeans and a sweatshirt came up and stood beside me. His face was smudged and abraded; his clothing was smeared with dirt and what looked to be blood; he held his left elbow gingerly in the palm of his hand. "You were asking about Dan?" he said.

So that was the anonymous caller's name. "Yes. Did he get out okay?"

"I don't think he was at home. At least, I saw him over at the Green around quarter to five."

"He was at home. I was talking with him on the phone when the quake hit."

"Oh, Jesus." The man s face paled under the smudges. "My name's Mel; I live . . . lived next door. Are you a friend of Dan's?"

"Yes," I said, realizing it was true.

"That's a surprise." He stared worriedly at the place where the two buildings leaned together.

"Why?"

"I thought Dan didn't have any friends left. He's pushed us away ever since the accident."

"Accident?"

65

"You must be a new friend, or else you'd know. Dan's woman was killed on the freeway last spring. A truck crushed her car."

The word "crushed" seemed to hang in the air between us. I said, "I've got to try to get him out of there," and stepped over the flattened portion of the fence.

Mel said, "I'll go with you."

I looked skeptically at his injured arm.

"It's nothing, really," he told me. "I was helping an old lady out of my building, and a beam grazed me."

"Well —" I broke off as a hail of debris came from the building to the left.

Without further conversation, Mel and I crossed the small front yard, skirting fallen bricks, broken glass, and jagged chunks of wallboard. Dusk was coming on fast now; here in the shadows of the leaning buildings it was darker than on the street. I moved toward where the cottage's front door should have been, but couldn't locate it. The windows, with their protruding grillwork, were impassable.

I said, "Is there another entrance?"

"In the back, off a little service porch."

I glanced to either side. The narrow passages between the cottage and the adjacent buildings were jammed with debris. I could possibly scale the mound at the right, but I was leery of setting up vibrations that might cause more debris to come tumbling down.

Mel said, "You'd better give it up. The way the cottage looks, I doubt he survived."

But I wasn't willing to give it up — not yet. There must be a way to at least locate Dan, see if he was alive. But how?

And then I remembered something else from our phone conversations. . . .

I said, "I'm going back there."

"Let me."

"No, stay here. That mound will support my weight, but not yours." I moved toward the side of the cottage before Mel could remind me of the risk I was taking.

The mound was over five feet high. I began to climb cautiously, testing every hand- and foothold. Twice jagged chunks of stucco cut my fingers; a piece of wood left a line of splinters on the back of my hand. When I neared the top, I heard the roar of a helicopter, its rotors flapping overhead. I froze, afraid that the air currents would precipitate more debris, then scrambled down the other side of the mound into a weed-choked backyard.

As I straightened, automatically brushing dirt from my jeans, my foot slipped on the soft, spongy ground, then sank into a puddle, probably a water main was broken nearby. The helicopter still hovered overhead; I couldn't hear a thing above its racket. Nor could I see much: it was even darker back here. I stood still until my eyes adjusted.

The cottage was not so badly damaged at its rear. The steps to the porch had collapsed and the rear wall leaned inward, but I could make out a door frame opening into blackness inside. I glanced up in irritation at the helicopter, saw it was going away. Waited, and then listened . . .

And heard what I had been hoping to. The music was now Beethoven — his third symphony, the *Eroica*. Its strains were muted, tinny. Music played by an out-of-area FM station, coming from a transistor radio. A transistor whose batteries were functioning long after the electricity had cut out. Whose batteries might have outlived its owner.

I moved quickly to the porch, grasped the iron rail beside the collapsed steps, and pulled myself up. I still could see nothing inside the cottage. The strains of the *Eroica* contin-

67

ued to pour forth, close by now.

Reflexively I reached into my purse for the small flash-light I usually kept there, then remembered it was at home on the kitchen counter — a reminder for me to replace its weak batteries. I swore softly, then started through the doorway, calling out to Dan.

No answer.

"Dan!"

This time I heard a groan.

I rushed forward into the blackness, following the sound of the music. After a few feet I came up against something solid, banging my shins. I lowered a hand, felt around. It was a wooden beam, wedged crosswise.

"Dan?"

Another groan. From the floor — perhaps under the beam. I squatted and made a wide sweep with my hands. They encountered a wool-clad arm; I slid my fingers down it until I touched the wrist, felt for the pulse. It was strong, although slightly irregular.

"Dan," I said, leaning closer, "it's Sharon, from the hot-line. We've got to get you out of here."

"Unh, Sharon?" His voice was groggy, confused. He'd probably been drifting in and out of consciousness since the beam fell on him.

"Can you move?" I asked.

". . . Something on my legs."

"Do they feel broken?"

"No, just pinned."

"I can't see much, but I'm going to try to move this beam off you. When I do, roll out from under."

". . . Okay."

From the position at which the beam was wedged, I could tell it would have to be raised. Balancing on the balls of my feet, I got a good grip on it and shoved upward with all my strength. It moved about six inches and then slipped from my grasp. Dan grunted.

"Are you all right?"

"Yeah. Try it again."

I stood, grasped it, and pulled this time. It yielded a little more, and I heard Dan slide across the floor. "I'm clear," he said — and just in time, because I once more lost my grip. The beam crashed down, setting up a vibration that made plaster fall from the ceiling.

"We've got to get out of here fast," I said. "Give me your hand."

He slipped it into mine — long-fingered, work-roughened. Quickly we went through the door, crossed the porch, jumped to the ground. The radio continued to play forlornly behind us. I glanced briefly at Dan, couldn't make out much more than a tall, slender build and a thatch of pale hair. His face turned from me, toward the cottage.

"Jesus," he said in an awed voice.

I tugged urgently at his hand. "There's no telling how long those apartment buildings are going to stand."

He turned, looked up at them, said "Jesus" again. I urged him toward the mound of debris.

This time I opted for speed rather than caution — a mistake, because as we neared the top, a cracking noise came from high above. I gave Dan a push, slid after him. A dark, jagged object hurtled down, missing us only by inches. More plaster board — deadly at that velocity.

For a moment I sat straddle-legged on the ground, sucking in my breath, releasing it tremulously, gasping for more air. Then hands pulled me to my feet and dragged me across the yard toward the sidewalk — Mel and Dan.

Night had fallen by now. A fire had broken out in the

house across the street. Its red-orange flickering showed the man I'd just rescued: ordinary-looking, with regular features that were now marred by dirt and a long cut on the forehead, from which blood had trickled and dried. His pale eyes were studying me; suddenly he looked abashed and shoved both hands into his jeans pocket.

After a moment he asked, "How did you find me?"

"I put together some of the things you'd said on the phone. Doesn't matter now."

"Why did you even bother?"

"Because I care."

He looked at the ground.

I added, "There never was any assault rifle, was there?"

He shook his head.

"You made it up, so someone would pay attention."

". . . Yeah."

I felt anger welling up — irrational, considering the present circumstances, but nonetheless justified. "You didn't have to frighten the people at the hotline. All you had to do was ask them for help. Or ask friends like Mel. He cares. People do, you know."

"Nobody does."

"Enough of that! All you have to do is look around to see how much people care about each other. Look at your friend here." I gestured at Mel, who was standing a couple feet away, staring at us. "He hurt his arm rescuing an old lady from his apartment house. Look at those people over by the burning house — they're doing everything they can to help the firefighters. All over this city people are doing things for one another. Goddamn it, I'd never laid eyes on you, but I risked my life anyway!"

Dan was silent for a long moment. Finally he looked up at me. "I know you did. What can I do in return?"

"For me? Nothing. Just pass it on to someone else."

Dan stared across the street at the flaming building, looked back into the shadows where his cottage lay in ruins. Then he nodded and squared his shoulders. To Mel he said, "Let's go over there, see if there's anything we can do."

He put his arm around my shoulders and hugged me briefly, then he and Mel set off at a trot.

The city is recovering now, as it did in 1906, and as it doubtless will when the next big quake hits. Resiliency is what disaster teaches us, I guess — along with the preciousness of life, no matter how disappointing or burdensome it may often seem.

Dan's recovering, too: he's only called the hotline twice, once for a referral to a therapist, and once to ask for my home number so he could invite me to dinner. I turned the invitation down, because neither of us needs to dwell on the trauma of October seventeenth, and I was fairly sure I heard a measure of relief in his voice when I did so.

I'll never forget Dan, though — or where I was when. And the strains of Beethoven's Third Symphony will forever remind me of the day after which things would never be the same again.

Dust to Dust

The dust was particularly bad on Monday, July sixth. It rose from the second floor where the demolition was going on and hung in the dry air of the photo lab. The trouble was, it didn't stay suspended. It settled on the formica counter tops, in the stainless-steel sink, on the plastic I'd covered the enlarger with. And worst of all, it settled on the negatives drying in the supposedly airtight cabinet.

The second time I checked the negatives I gave up. They'd have to be soaked for hours to get the dust out of the emulsion. And when I rehung them they'd only be coated with the stuff again.

I turned off the orange safelight and went into the studio. A thick film of powder covered everything there too. I'd had the foresight to put my cameras away, but somehow the dust crept into the cupboards, through the leather cases and onto the lenses themselves. The restoration project was turning into a nightmare, and it had barely begun.

I crossed the studio to the Victorian's big front windows. The city of Phoenix sprawled before me, skyscrapers shimmering in the heat. Camelback Mountain rose out of the flat land to the right, and the oasis of Encanto Park beckoned at the left. I could drive over there and sit under a tree by the water. I could rent a paddlewheel boat. Anything to escape the dry grit-laden heat.

But I had to work on the photos for the book.

And I couldn't work on them because I couldn't get the

negatives to come out clear.

I leaned my forehead against the window frame, biting back my frustration.

"Jane!" My name echoed faintly from below. "Jane! Come down here!"

It was Roy, the workman I'd hired to demolish the rabbit warren of cubicles that had been constructed when the Victorian was turned into a rooming house in the thirties. The last time he'd shouted for me like that was because he'd discovered a stained-glass window preserved intact between two false walls. My spirits lifting, I hurried down the winding stairs.

The second floor was a wasteland heaped with debris. Walls leaned at crazy angles. Piles of smashed plaster blocked the hall. Rough beams and lath were exposed. The air was even worse down there — full of powder which caught in my nostrils and covered my clothing whenever I brushed against anything.

I called back to Roy, but his answering shout came from further below, in the front hall.

I descended the stairs into the gloom, keeping to the wall side because the bannister was missing. Roy stood, crowbar in hand, at the rear of the stairway. He was a tall, thin man with a pockmarked face and curly black hair, a drifter who had wandered into town willing to work cheap so long as no questions were asked about his past. Roy, along with his mongrel dog, now lived in his truck in my driveway. In spite of his odd appearance and stealthy comings and goings, I felt safer having him around while living in a half-demolished house.

Now he pushed up the goggles he wore to keep the plaster out of his eyes and waved the crowbar toward the stairs.

"Jane, I've really found something this time." His voice

trembled. Roy had a genuine enthusiasm for old houses, and this house in particular.

I hurried down the hall and looked under the stairs. The plaster-and-lath had been partially ripped off and tossed onto the floor. Behind it, I could see only darkness. The odor of dry rot wafted out of the opening.

Dammit, now there was debris in the downstairs hall too. "I thought I told you to finish the second floor before you started here."

"But take a look."

"I am. I see a mess."

"No, here. Take the flashlight. Look."

I took it and shone it through the hole. It illuminated gold-patterned wallpaper and wood paneling. My irritation vanished. "What is it, do you suppose?"

"I think it's what they call a 'cozy.' A place where they hung coats and ladies left their outside boots when they came calling." He shouldered past me. "Let's get a better look."

I backed off and watched as he tugged at the wall with the crowbar, the muscles in his back and arms straining. In minutes, he had ripped a larger section off. It crashed to the floor and when the dust cleared I shone the light once more.

It was a paneled nook with a bench and ornate brass hooks on the wall. "I think you're right — it's a cozy."

Roy attacked the wall once more and soon the opening was clear. He stepped inside, the leg of his jeans catching on a nail. "It's big enough for three people." His voice echoed in the empty space.

"Why do you think they sealed it up?" I asked.

"Fire regulations, when they converted to a rooming house. They . . . what's this?"

I leaned forward.

Roy turned, his hand outstretched. I looked at the object resting on his palm and recoiled.

"God!"

"Take it easy." He stepped out of the cozy. "It's only a dead bird."

It was small, probably a sparrow, and like the stained-glass window Roy had found the past week, perfectly preserved.

"Ugh!" I said. "How did it get in there?"

Roy stared at the small body in fascination. "It's probably been there since the wall was constructed. Died of hunger, or lack of air."

I shivered. "But it's not rotted."

"In this dry climate? It's like mummification. You could preserve a body for decades."

"Put it down. It's probably diseased."

He shrugged. "I doubt it." But he stepped back into the cozy and placed it on the bench. Then he motioned for the flashlight. "The wallpaper's in good shape. And the wood looks like golden oak. And . . . hello."

"Now what?"

He bent over and picked something up. "It's a comb, a mother-of-pearl comb like ladies wore in their hair." He held it out. The comb had long teeth to sweep up heavy tresses on a woman's head.

"This place never ceases to amaze me." I took it and brushed off the plaster dust. Plaster . . . "Roy, this wall couldn't have been put up in the thirties."

"Well the building permit shows the house was converted then."

"But the rest of the false walls are fireproof sheetrock, like regulations required. This one is plaster-and-lath. This cozy has been sealed off longer than that. Maybe since ladies wore this kind of comb."

"Maybe." His eyes lit up. "We've found an eighty-year-old bird mummy."

"I guess so." The comb fascinated me, as the bird had Roy. I stared at it.

"You should get shots of this for your book," Roy said.

"What?"

"Your book."

I shook my head, disoriented. Of course — the book. It was defraying the cost of the renovation, a photo essay on restoring one of Phoenix's grand old ladies.

"You haven't forgotten the book?" Roy's tone was mocking.

I shook my head again. "Roy, why did you break down this wall? When I told you to finish upstairs first?"

"Look, if you're pissed off about the mess . . ."

"No, I'm curious. Why?"

Now he looked confused. "I . . ."

"Yes?"

"I don't know."

"Don't know?"

He frowned, his pockmarked face twisting in concentration. "I really *don't* know. I had gone to the kitchen for a beer and I came through here and . . . I don't know."

I watched him thoughtfully, clutching the mother-of-pearl comb. "Okay," I finally said, "just don't start on a new area again without checking with me."

"Sorry. I'll clean up this mess."

"Not yet. Let me get some photos first." Still holding the comb, I went up to the studio to get a camera.

In the week that followed, Roy attacked the second floor with a vengeance and it began to take on its original floorplan. He made other discoveries — nothing as spectacular as the cozy, but interesting — old newspapers, coffee cans of a brand not sold in decades, a dirty pair of baby booties. I photographed each faithfully and assured my publisher that the work was going well.

It wasn't, though. As Roy worked, the dust increased and my frustration with the book project — not to mention the commercial jobs that were my bread and butter — deepened. The house, fortunately, was paid for, purchased with a bequest from my aunt, the only member of my family who didn't think it dreadful for a girl from Fairmont, West Virginia, to run off and become a photographer in a big western city. The money from the book, however, was what would make the house habitable, and the first part of the advance had already been eaten up. The only way I was going to squeeze more cash out of the publisher was to show him some progess, and so far I had made none of that.

Friday morning I told Roy to take the day off. Maybe I could get some work done if he wasn't raising clouds of dust. I spent the morning in the lab developing the rolls I'd shot that week, then went into the studio and looked over what prints I had ready to show to the publisher.

The exterior shots, taken before the demolition had begun, were fine. They showed a three-story structure with square bay windows and rough peeling paint. The fanlight over the front door had been broken and replaced with plywood, and much of the gingerbread trim was missing. All in all, she was a bedraggled old lady, but she would again be beautiful — if I could finish the damned book.

The early interior shots were not bad either. In fact, they evoked a nice sense of gloomy neglect. And the renovation of this floor, the attic, into studio and lab was well documented. It was with the second floor that my problems began.

At first the dust had been slight, and I hadn't noticed it on the negatives. As a result the prints were marred with white specks. In a couple of cases the dust had scratched the negatives while I'd handled them and the fine lines showed up in the pictures. Touching them up would be painstaking work but it could be done.

But now the dust had become more active, taken over. I was forced to soak and resoak the negatives. A few rolls of film had proven unsalvageable after repeated soakings. And, in losing them, I was losing documentation of a very important part of the renovation.

I went to the window and looked down at the driveway where Roy was sunning himself on the grass beside his truck. The mongrel dog lay next to a tire in the shade of the vehicle. Roy reached under there for one of his everpresent beers, swigged at it and set it back down.

How, I wondered, did he stand the heat? He took to it like a native, seemingly oblivious to the sun's glare. But then, maybe Roy *was* a native of the Sun Belt. What did I know of him, really?

Only that he was a tireless worker and his knowledge of old houses was invaluable to me. He unerringly sensed which were the original walls and which were false, what should be torn down and what should remain. He could tell whether a fixture was the real thing or merely a good copy. I could not have managed without him.

I shrugged off thoughts of my handyman and lifted my hair from my shoulders. It was wheat colored, heavy and, right now, uncomfortable. I pulled it on top of my head, looked around and spotted the mother-of-pearl comb we'd found in the cozy. It was small, designed to be worn as half of a pair on one side of the head. I secured the hair on my left with it, then pinned up the right side with one of the clips I used to hang negatives. Then I went into the dark-room.

The negatives were dry. I took one strip out of the cabinet and held it to the light. It seemed relatively clear. Perhaps, as long as the house wasn't disturbed, the dust ceased its silent takeover. I removed the other strips. Dammit, some were still spotty, especially those of the cozy and the objects we'd discovered in it. Those could be reshot, however. I decided to go ahead and make contact prints of the lot.

I cut the negatives into strips of six frames each, then inserted them in plastic holders. Shutting the door and turning on the safelight, I removed photographic paper from the small refrigerator, placed it and the negative holders under glass in the enlarger, and set my timer. Nine seconds at f/8 would do nicely.

When the first sheet of paper was exposed, I slipped it into the developer tray and watched, fascinated as I had been since the first time I'd done this, for the images to emerge. Yes, nine seconds had been right. I went to the enlarger and exposed the other negatives.

I moved the contact sheets along, developer to stop bath to fixer, then put them into the washing tray. Now I could open the door to the darkroom and let some air in. Even though Roy had insulated up here, it was still hot and close when I was working in the lab. I pinned my hair more securely on my head and took the contact sheets to the print dryer.

I scanned the sheets eagerly as they came off the roller. Most of the negatives had printed clearly and some of the shots were quite good. I should be able to assemble a decent selection for my editor with very little trouble. Relieved, I reached for the final sheet.

There were the pictures I had shot the day we'd discovered the cozy. They were different from the others. And different from past dust-damaged rolls. I picked up my magnifying loupe and took the sheet out into the light.

Somehow the dust had gotten to this set of negatives. Rather than leaving speckles, though, it had drifted like a sandstorm. It clustered in iridescent patches, as if an object had caught the light in a strange way. The effect was eerie; perhaps I could put it to use.

I circled the oddest-looking frames and went back into the darkroom, shutting the door securely. I selected the negative that corresponded to one circled on the sheet, routinely sprayed it with canned air for surface dirt and inserted it into the holder of the enlarger. Adjusting the height, I shone the light down through the negative, positioning the image within the paper guides.

Yes, I had something extremely odd here.

Quickly I snapped off the light, set the timer and slipped a piece of unexposed paper into the guides. The light came on again, the timer whirred and then all was silent and dark. I slid the paper into the developer tray and waited.

The image was of the cozy with the bird mummy resting on the bench. That would have been good enough, but the effect of the dust made it spectacular. Above the dead bird rose a white-gray shape, a second bird in flight, spiraling upward.

Like a ghost. The ghost of a trapped bird, finally freed.

I shivered.

Could I use something like this in the book? It was perfect. But what if my editor asked how I'd done it? Photography was not only art but science. You strove for images that evoked certain emotions. But you had damned well better know how you got those images.

Don't worry about that now, I told myself. See what else is here.

I replaced the bird negative with another one and exposed it. The image emerged slowly in the developing tray: first the carved arch of the cozy, then the plaster-and-lath heaped on the floor, finally the shimmering figure of a man.

I leaned over the tray. Roy? A double exposure perhaps? It looked like Roy, yet it didn't. And I hadn't taken any pictures of him anyway. No, this was another effect created by the dust, a mere outline of a tall man in what appeared to be an old-fashioned frock coat.

The ghost of a man? That was silly. I didn't believe in such things. Not in *my* house.

Still, the photos had a wonderful eeriness. I could include them in the book, as a novelty chapter. I could write a little explanation about the dust.

And while on the subject of dust, wasn't it rising again? Had Roy begun work, even though I'd told him not to?

I crossed the studio to the window and looked down. No, he was still there by the truck, although he was now dappled by the shade of a nearby tree. The sun had moved; it was getting on toward midafternoon.

Back in the darkroom I continued to print from the dust-damaged group of negatives. Maybe I was becoming fanciful, or maybe the chemicals were getting to me after being cooped up in here all day, but I was seeing stranger and stranger images. One looked like a woman in a long, full-skirted dress, standing in the entrance to the cozy. In another the man was reaching out — maybe trying to catch the bird that had invaded his home?

Was it his home? Who were these people? What were

81

they doing in my negatives?

As I worked the heat increased. I became aware of the dust which, with or without Roy's help, had again taken up its stealthy activity. It had a life all its own, as demonstrated by these photos. I began to worry that it would damage the prints before I could put them on the dryer.

The gritty air became suffocating. The clip that held my hair on the right side came loose and a lock hung hot and heavy against my neck. I put one last print on the dryer and went into the studio.

Dust lay on every surface again. What had caused it to rise? I went to the window and looked down. Roy was sitting on the bed of the truck with the mongrel, drinking another beer. Well, if he hadn't done anything, I was truly stumped. Was I going to be plagued by dust throughout the restoration, whether work was going on or not?

I began to pace the studio, repinning my hair and securing the mother-of-pearl comb as I went. The eerie images had me more disturbed than I was willing to admit. And this dust . . . dammit, this *dust!*

Anger flaring, I headed down the stairs. I'd get to the bottom of this. There had to be a perfectly natural cause, and if I had to turn the house upside down I'd find it.

The air on the second floor was choking, but the dust seemed to rise from the first. I charged down the next flight of stairs, unheedful for the first time since I'd lived here of the missing bannister. The dust seemed thickest by the cozy. Maybe opening the wall had created a draft. I hurried back there.

A current of air, cooler than that in the hall, emanated from the cozy. I stepped inside and felt around with my hand. It came from a crack in the bench. A crack? I knelt to examine it. No, it wasn't a crack. It looked like the seat of the bench was designed to be lifted. Of course it was — there were hidden hinges which we'd missed when we first discovered it.

I grasped the edge of the bench and pulled. It was stuck. I tugged harder. Still it didn't give. Feeling along the seat, I found the nails that held it shut.

This called for Roy's strength. I went to the front door and called him. "Bring your crowbar. We're about to make another discovery."

He stood up in the bed of the truck and rummaged through his tools, then came toward me, crowbar in hand. "What now?"

"The cozy. That bench in there has a seat that raises. Some sort of woodbox, maybe."

Roy stopped inside the front door. "Now that you mention it, I think you're right. It's not a woodbox, though. In the old days, ladies would change into house shoes from outdoor shoes when they came calling. The bench was to store them in."

"Well, it's going to be my woodbox. And I think it's what's making the dust move around so much. There's a draft coming from it." I led him back to the cozy. "How come you know so much about old houses anyway?"

He shrugged. "When you've torn up as many as I have, you learn fast. I've always had an affinity for Victorians. What do you want me to do here?"

"It's nailed shut. Pry it open."

"I might wreck the wood."

"Pry gently."

"I'll try."

I stepped back and let him at the bench. He worked carefully, loosening each nail with the point of the bar. It seemed to take a long time. Finally he turned.

"There. All the nails are out."

"Then open it."

"No, it's your discovery. You do it." He stepped back.

The draft was stronger now. I went up to the bench, then hesitated.

"Go on," Roy said. His voice shook with excitement.

My palms were sweaty. Grit stuck to them. I reached out and lifted the seat.

My sight was blurred by a duststorm like those on the negatives. Then it cleared. I leaned forward. Recoiled. A scream rose in my throat, but it came out a croak.

It was the lady of my photographs.

She lay on her back inside the bench. She wore a long, full-skirted dress of some beaded material. Her hands were crossed on her breasts. Like the bird mummy, she was perfectly preserved — even to the heavy wheat-colored hair, with the mother-of-pearl comb holding it up on the left side.

I put my hand to *my* wheat-colored hair. To *my* mother-of-pearl comb. Then, shaken, I turned to Roy.

He had raised the arm that held the crowbar — just like the man had had his hand raised in the last print, the one I'd forgotten to remove from the dryer. Roy's work shirt billowed out, resembling an old-fashioned frock coat. The look in his eyes was eerie.

And the dust was rising again . . .

Forbidden Things

All the years that I was growing up in a poor suburb of Los Angeles, my mother would tell me stories of the days I couldn't remember when we lived with my father on the wild north coast. She'd tell of a gray, misty land suddenly made brilliant by quicksilver flashes off the sea; of white-sand beaches that would disappear in a storm, then emerge strewn with driftwood and treasures from foreign shores; of a deeply forested ridge of hills where, so the Pomo Indians claimed, spirits walked by night.

Our cabin nestled on that ridge, high above the little town of Camel Rock and the humpbacked offshore mass that inspired its name. The cabin, built to last by my handyman father, was of local redwood, its foundation sunk deep in bedrock. There was a woodstove and home-woven curtains. There were stained-glass windows and a sleeping loft; there was . . .

Although I had no recollection of the place we'd left when I was two, it somehow seemed more real to me than our shabby pink bungalow with the cracked sidewalk out front and the packed-dirt yard out back. I'd lie in bed late at night feeling the heat from the woodstove, watching the light as it filtered through the stained-glass panels, listening to the wind buffet our secure aerie. I was sure I could smell my mother's baking bread, hear the deep rumble of my father's voice. But no matter how hard I tried, I could not call up the image of my father's face, even though a stiff and formal studio portrait of him sat on our coffee table.

When I asked my mother why she and I had left a place of quicksilver days and night-walking spirits, she'd grow quiet. When I asked where my father was now, she'd turn away. As I grew older I realized there were shadows over our departure — shadows in which forbidden things stood still and silent.

Is it any wonder that when my mother died — young, at forty-nine, but life hadn't been kind to her and heart trouble ran in the family — is it any wonder that I packed everything I cared about and went back to the place of my birth to confront those forbidden things?

I'd located Camel Rock on the map when I was nine, tracing the coast highway with my finger until it reached a jutting point of land north of Fort Bragg. Once this had been logging country — hardy men working the crosscut saw and jackscrew in the forests, bull teams dragging their heavy loads to the coast, fresh-cut logs thundering down the chutes to schooners that lay at anchor in the coves below. But by the time I was born, lumbering was an endangered industry. Today, I knew, the voice of the chain saw was stilled and few logging trucks rumbled along the highway. Legislation to protect the environment, coupled with a severe construction slump, had all but killed the old economy. Instead new enterprises had sprung up: wineries; mushroom, garlic, and herb farms; tourist shops and bed-and-breakfasts. These were only marginally profitable, however; the north coast was financially strapped.

I decided to go anyway.

It was a good time for me to leave southern California. Two failed attempts at college, a ruined love affair, a series of slipping-down jobs — all argued for radical change. I'd had no family except my mother; even my cat had died the previous October. As I gave notice at the coffee shop where I'd been waitressing, disposed of the contents of the bungalow, and turned the keys back to the landlord, I said no goodbyes. Yet I left with hope of a welcome. Maybe there would be a place for me in Camel Rock. Maybe someone would even remember my family and fill in the gaps in my early life.

I know now that I was really hoping for a reunion with my father.

Mist blanketed the coast the afternoon I drove my old Pinto over the bridge spanning the mouth of the Deer River and into Camel Rock. Beyond sandstone cliffs the sea lay flat and seemingly motionless. The town — a strip of buildings on either side of the highway, with dirt lanes straggling up toward the hills — looked deserted. A few drifting columns of wood smoke, some lighted signs in shop windows, a hunched and bundled figure walking along the shoulder — these were the only signs of life. I drove slowly, taking it all in: a supermarket, some bars, a little mall full of tourist shops. Post office, laundromat, defunct real estate agency, old sagging hotel that looked to be the only lodging place. When I'd gone four blocks and passed the last gas station and the cable TV company, I ran out of town; I U-turned, went back to the hotel, and parked my car between two pickups out front.

For a moment I sat behind the wheel, feeling flat. The town didn't look like the magical place my mother had described; if anything, it was seedier than the suburb I'd left yesterday. I had to force myself to get out, and when I did, I stood beside the Pinto, staring up at the hotel. Pale green with once white trim, all of it blasted and faded by the elements. An inscription above its front door gave the date it was built — 1879, the height of last century's logging boom. Neon beer signs flashed in its lower windows; gulls perched along the peak of its roof, their droppings splashed over the steps and front porch. I watched as one soared in for a landing, crying shrilly. Sea breeze ruffled my short blond hair, and I smelled fish and brine.

The smell of the sea had always delighted me. Now it triggered a sense of connection to this place. I thought: *Home*.

The thought lent me the impetus to take out my overnight bag and carried me over the threshold of the hotel. Inside was a dim lobby that smelled of dust and cat. I peered through the gloom but saw no one. Loud voices came from a room to the left, underscored by the clink of glasses and the thump and clatter of dice-rolling; I went over, looked in, and saw an old-fashioned tavern, peopled mainly by men in work clothes. The ship's clock that hung crooked behind the bar said four-twenty. Happy hour got under way early in Camel Rock.

There was a public phone on the other side of the lobby. I crossed to it and opened the thin county directory, aware that my fingers were trembling. No listing for my father. No listing for anyone with my last name. More disappointed than I had any right to be, I replaced the book and turned away.

Just then a woman came out of a door under the steep staircase. She was perhaps in her early sixties, tall and gaunt, with tightly permed gray curls and a faced lined by weariness. When she saw me, her pale eyes registered surprise. "May I help you?"

I hesitated, the impulse to flee the shabby hotel and drive away from Camel Rock nearly irresistible. Then I thought: Come on, give the place a chance. "Do you have a room available?"

"We've got nothing *but* available rooms." She smiled wryly and got a card for me to fill out. Lacking any other, I put down my old address and formed the letters of my signature — Ashley Heikkinen — carefully. I'd always hated my last name; it seemed graceless and misshapen beside my first. Now I was glad it was unusual; maybe someone here in town would recognize it. The woman glanced disinterestedly at the card, however, then turned away and studied a rack of keys.

"Front room or back room?"

"Which is more quiet?"

"Well, in front you've got the highway noise, but there's not much traffic at night. In the back you've got the boys" — she motioned at the door to the tavern — "Scrapping in the parking lot at closing time."

Just what I wanted — a room above a bar frequented by quarrelsome drunks. "I guess I'll take the front."

The woman must have read my expression. "Oh, honey, don't you worry about them. They're not so bad, but there's nobody as contentious as an out-of-work logger who's had one over his limit."

I smiled and offered my Visa card. She shook her head and pointed to a Cash Only sign. I dug in my wallet and came up with the amount she named. It wasn't much, but I didn't have much to begin with. There had been a small life insurance policy on my mother, but most of it had gone toward burying her. If I was to stay in Camel Rock, I'd need a job.

"Are a lot of people around here out of work?" I asked as the woman wrote up a receipt.

"Loggers, mostly. The type who won't bite the bullet and learn another trade. But the rest of us aren't in much better shape."

"Have you heard of any openings for a waitress or a bartender?"

"For yourself?"

"Yes. If I can find a job, I may settle here."

Her hand paused over the receipt book. "Honey, why on earth would you want to do that?"

"I was born here. Maybe you knew my parents — Melinda and John Heikkinen?"

She shook her head and tore the receipt from the book. "My husband and me, we just moved down here last year from Del Norte County — things're even worse up there, believe me. We bought this hotel because it was cheap and we thought we could make a go of it."

"Have you?"

"Not really. We don't have the wherewithal to fix it up, so we can't compete with the new motels or bed-and-breakfasts. And we made the mistake of giving bar credit to the locals."

"That's too bad," I said. "There must be some jobs available, though. I'm a good waitress, a fair bartender. And I . . . like people," I added lamely.

She smiled, the lines around her eyes crinkling kindly. I guessed she'd presented meager credentials a time or two herself. "Well, I suppose you could try over at the mall. I hear Barbie Cannon's been doing real good with her Beachcomber Shop, and the tourist season'll be here before we know it. Maybe she can use some help."

I thanked her and took the room key she offered, but as I picked up my bag I thought of something else. "Is there a newspaper in town?"

"As far as I know, there never has been. There's one of those little county shoppers, but it doesn't have ads for jobs, if that's what you're after."

"Actually, I'm trying to locate . . . a family member. I thought if there was a newspaper, I could look through their back issues. What about longtime residents of the town? Is there anybody who's an amateur historian, for instance?"

"Matter of fact, there is. Gus Galick. Lives on his fishing trawler, the *Irma*, down at the harbor. Comes in here regular."

"How long has he lived here?"

"All his life."

Just the person I wanted to talk with.

The woman added, "Gus is away this week, took a charter party down the coast. I think he said he'd be back next Thursday."

Another disappointment. I swallowed it, told myself the delay would give me time to settle in and get to know the place of my birth. And I'd start by visiting the Beachcomber Shop.

The shop offered exactly the kind of merchandise its name implied: seashells; driftwood; inexpert carvings of gulls, grebes, and sea lions. Postcards and calendars and T-shirts and paperback guidebooks. Shell jewelry, paperweights, ceramic whales and dolphins. Nautical toys and candles and wind chimes. All of it was totally predictable, but the woman who popped up from behind the counter was anything but.

She was very tall, well over six feet, and her black hair stood up in long, stiff spikes. A gold ring pierced her left nostril, and several others hung from either earlobe. She wore a black leather tunic with metal studs, over lacy black tights and calf-high boots. In L.A. I wouldn't have given her a second glance, but this was Camel Rock. Such people weren't supposed to happen here.

The woman watched my reaction, then threw back her head and laughed throatily. I felt a blush begin to creep over my face.

"Hey, don't worry about it," she told me. "You should see how I scare the little bastards who drag their parents in here, whining about how they absolutely *have* to have a blow-up Willie the Whale."

"Ah, isn't that bad for business?"

"Hell, no. Embarrasses the parents, and they buy twice as much as they would've."

"Oh."

"So — what can I do for you?"

"I'm looking for Barbie Cannon."

"You found her." She flopped onto a stool next to the counter, stretching out her long legs.

"My name's Ashley Heikkinen." I watched her face for some sign of recognition. There wasn't any, but that didn't surprise me; Barbie Cannon was only a few years older than I — perhaps thirty — and too young to remember a family that had left so long ago. Besides, she didn't look as if she'd been born and raised here.

"I'm looking for a job," I went on, "and the woman at the hotel said you might need some help in the shop."

She glanced around at the merchandise that was heaped haphazardly on the shelves and spilled over onto the floor here and there. "Well, Penny's right — I probably do." Then she looked back at me. "You're not local."

"I just came up from L.A."

"Me too, about a year ago. There're a fair number of us transplants, and the division between us and the locals is pretty clear-cut."

"How so?"

"A lot of the natives are down on their luck, resentful of

the newcomers, especially ones like me, who're doing well. Oh, some of them're all right; they understand that the only way for the area to survive is to restructure the economy. But most of them are just sitting around the bars mumbling about how the spotted owl ruined their lives and hoping the timber industry'll make a comeback — and that ain't gonna happen. So why're *you* here?"

"I was born in Camel Rock. And I'm sick of southern California."

"So you decided to get back to your roots."

"In a way."

"You alone?"

I nodded.

"Got a place to stay?"

"The hotel, for now."

"Well, it's not so bad, and Penny'll extend credit if you run short. As for a job . . ." She paused, looking around again. "You know, I came up here thinking I'd work on my photography. The next Ansel Adams and all that." She grinned self-mockingly. "Trouble is, I got to be such a successful businesswoman that I don't even have time to load my camera. Tell you what — why don't we go over to the hotel tavern, tilt a few, talk it over?"

"Why not?" I said.

Mist hugged the tops of the sequoias and curled in tendrils around their trunks. The mossy ground under my feet was damp and slick. I hugged my hooded sweatshirt against the chill and moved cautiously up the incline from where I'd left the car on an overgrown logging road. My soles began to slip, and I crouched, catching at a stump for balance. The wet fronds of a fern brushed my cheek.

I'd been tramping through the hills for over two hours,

searching every lane and dirt track for the burned-out cabin that Barbie Cannon had photographed shortly after her arrival in Camel Rock last year. Barbie had invited me to her place for dinner the night before after we'd agreed on the terms of my new part-time job, and in the course of the evening she'd shown me her portfolio of photographs. One, a grainy black-and-white image of a ruin, so strongly affected me that I'd barely been able to sleep. This morning I'd dropped by the shop and gotten Barbie to draw me a map of where she'd found it, but her recollection was so vague that I might as well have had no map at all.

I pushed back to my feet and continued climbing. The top of the rise was covered by a dense stand of sumac and bay laurel; the spicy scent of the laurel leaves mixed with stronger odors of redwood and eucalyptus. The mixed bouquet triggered the same sense of connection that I'd felt as I stood in front of the hotel the previous afternoon. I breathed deeply, then elbowed through the dense branches.

From the other side of the thicket I looked down on a sloping meadow splashed with the brilliant yellow-orange of California poppies. More sequoias crowned the ridge on its far side, and through their branches I caught a glimpse of the flat, leaden sea. A stronger feeling of familiarity stole over me. I remembered my mother saying, "In the spring, the meadow was full of poppies, and you could see the ocean from our front steps. . . ."

The mist was beginning to break up overhead. I watched a hawk circle against a patch of blue high above the meadow, then wheel and flap away toward the inland hills. He passed over my head, and I could feel the beating of his great wings. I turned, my gaze following his flight path —

And then I spotted the cabin, overgrown and wrapped in shadow, only yards away. Built into the downward slope of

94

the hill, its moss-covered foundations were anchored in bedrock, as I'd been told. But the rest was only blackened and broken timbers, a collapsed roof on whose shakes vegetation had taken root, a rusted stove chimney about to topple, empty windows and doors.

I drew in my breath and held it for a long moment. Then I slowly moved forward.

Stone steps, four of them. I counted as I climbed. Yes, you could still see the Pacific from here, the meadow too. And this opening was where the door had been. Beyond it, nothing but a concrete slab covered with debris. Plenty of evidence that picnickers had been here.

I stepped over the threshold.

One big empty room. Nothing left, not even the mammoth iron woodstove. Vines growing through the timbers, running across the floor. And at the far side, a collapsed heap of burned lumber — the sleeping loft?

Something crunched under my foot. I looked down, squatted, poked at it gingerly with my fingertip. Glass, green glass. It could have come from a picnicker's wine bottle. Or it could have come from a broken stained-glass window.

I stood, coldness upon my scalp and shoulder blades. Coldness that had nothing to do with the sea wind that bore the mist from the coast. I closed my eyes against the shadows and the ruin. Once again I could smell my mother's baking bread, hear my father's voice. Once again I thought: *Home*.

But when I opened my eyes, the warmth and light vanished. Now all I saw was the scene of a terrible tragedy.

"Barbie," I said, "What do you know about the Northcoast Lumber Company?"

She looked up from the box of wind chimes she was unpacking. "Used to be the big employer around here."

"Where do they have their offices? I couldn't find a listing in the county phone book."

"I hear they went bust in the eighties."

"Then why would they still own land up in the hills?"

"Don't know. Why?"

I hesitated. Yesterday, the day after I'd found the cabin, I'd driven down to the county offices at Fort Bragg and spent the entire afternoon poring over the land plats for this area. The place where the ruin stood appeared to belong to the lumber company. There was no reason I shouldn't confide in Barbie about my search, but something held me back. After a moment I said, "Oh, I saw some acreage that I might be interested in buying."

She raised her eyebrows; the extravagant white eye shadow and bright-red lipstick that she wore today made her look like an astonished clown. "On what I'm paying you for part-time work, you're buying land?"

"I've got some savings from my mom's life insurance." That much was true, but the small amount wouldn't buy even a square foot of land.

"Huh." She went back to her unpacking. "Well, I don't know for a fact that Northcoast did go bust. Penny told me that the owner's widow is still alive. Used to live on a big estate near here, but a long time ago she moved down the coast to that fancy retirement community at Timber Point. Maybe she could tell you about this acreage."

"What's her name, do you know?"

"No, but you could ask Penny. She and Gene bought the hotel from her."

"Madeline Carmichael," Penny said. "Lady in her late

fifties. She and her husband used to own a lot of property around here."

"You know her, then."

"Nope, never met her. Our dealings were through a realtor and her lawyer."

"She lives down at Timber Point?"

"Uh-huh. The realtor told us she's a recluse, never leaves her house and has everything she needs delivered."

"Why, do you suppose?"

"Why not? She can afford it. Oh, the realtor hinted that there's some tragedy in her past, but I don't put much stock in that. I'll tell you" — her tired eyes swept the dingy hotel lobby — "if I had a beautiful home and all that money, I'd never go out, either."

Madeline Carmichael's phone number and address were unlisted. When I drove down to Timber Point the next day, I found high grape-stake fences and a gatehouse; the guard told me that Mrs. Carmichael would see no one who wasn't on her visitors list. When I asked him to call her, he refused. "If she was expecting you," he said, "she'd have sent your name down."

Penny had given me the name of the realtor who handled the sale of the hotel. He put me in touch with Mrs. Carmichael's lawyer in Fort Bragg. The attorney told me he'd check about the ownership of the land and get back to me. When he did, his reply was terse: The land was part of the original Carmichael estate; title was held by the nearly defunct lumber company; it was not for sale.

So why had my parents built their cabin on the Carmichael estate? Were my strong feelings of connection to the burned-out ruin in the hills false?

Maybe, I told myself, it was time to stop chasing memories and start building a life for myself here in Camel Rock. Maybe it was best to leave the past alone.

The following weekend brought the kind of quicksilver days my mother had told me about, and in turn they lured tourists in record numbers. We couldn't restock the Beachcomber Shop's shelves fast enough. On the next Wednesday — Barbie's photography day — I was unpacking fresh merchandise and filling in where necessary while waiting for the woman Barbie bought her driftwood sculptures from to make a delivery. Business was slack in the late-afternoon hours; I moved slowly, my mind on what to wear to a dinner party being given that evening by some new acquaintances who ran an herb farm. When the bell over the door jangled, I started.

It was Mrs. Fleming, the driftwood lady. I recognized her by the big plastic wash basket of sculptures that she toted. A tiny white-haired woman, she seemed too frail for such a load. I moved to take it from her.

She resisted, surprisingly strong. Her eyes narrowed, and she asked, "Where's Barbie?"

"Wednesday's her day off."

"And who are you?"

"Ashley Heikkinen. I'm Barbie's part-time —"

"*What* did you say?"

"My name is Ashley Heikkinen. I just started here last week."

Mrs. Fleming set the basket on the counter and regarded me sternly, spots of red appearing on her cheeks. "Just what are you up to, young woman?"

"I don't understand."

"Why are you using that name?"

"Using . . . ? It's my name."

"It most certainly is not! This is a very cruel joke."

The woman had to be unbalanced. Patiently I said, "Look, my name really is Ashley Heikkinen. I was born in Camel Rock but moved away when I was two. I grew up outside Los Angeles, and when my mother died I decided to come back here."

Mrs. Fleming shook her head, her lips compressed, eyes glittering with anger.

"I can prove who I am," I added, reaching under the counter for my purse. "Here's my identification."

"Of course you'd have identification. Everyone knows how to obtain that under the circumstances."

"What circumstances?"

She turned and moved toward the door. "I can't imagine what you possibly expect to gain by this charade, young woman, but you can be sure I'll speak to Barbie about you."

"Please, wait!"

She pushed through the door, and the bell above it jangled harshly as it slammed shut. I hurried to the window and watched her cross the parking lot in a vigorous stride that belied her frail appearance. As she turned at the highway, I looked down and saw I had my wallet out, prepared to prove my identity.

Why, I wondered, did I feel compelled to justify my existence to this obviously deranged stranger?

The dinner party that evening was pleasant, and I returned to the hotel at a little after midnight with the fledgling sense of belonging that making friends in a strange place brings. The fog was in thick, drawn by hot inland temperatures. It put a gritty sheen on my face, and when I touched my tongue to my lips, I tasted the sea. I locked the Pinto and started across the rutted parking lot to the rear

99

entrance. Heavy footsteps came up behind me.

Conditioned by my years in L.A., I already held my car key in my right hand, tip out as a weapon. I glanced back and saw a stocky, bearded man bearing down on me. When I sidestepped and turned, he stopped, and his gaze moved to the key. He'd been drinking — beer, and plenty of it.

From the tavern, I thought. Probably came out to the parking lot because the rest room's in use and he couldn't wait. "After you," I said, opening the door for him.

He stepped inside the narrow, dim hallway. I let him get a ways ahead, then followed. The door stuck, and I turned to give it a tug. The man reversed, came up swiftly, and grasped my shoulder.

"Hey!" I said.

He spun me around and slammed me against the wall. "Lady, what the hell're you after?"

"Let go of me!" I pushed at him.

He pushed back, grabbed my other shoulder, and pinned me there. I stopped struggling, took a deep breath, told myself to remain calm.

"Not going to hurt you, lady," he said. "I just want to know what your game is."

Two lunatics in one day. "What do you mean — game?"

"My name is Ashley Heikkinen," he said in a falsetto, then dropped to his normal pitch. "Who're you trying to fool? And what's in it for you?"

"I don't —"

"Don't give me that! You might be able to stonewall an old lady like my mother —"

"Your mother?"

"Yeah, Janet Fleming. You expect her to believe you, for Christ's sake? What you did, you upset her plenty. She had to take one of the Valiums the doctor gave me for my bad back."

"I don't understand what your mother's problem is."

"Jesus, you're a cold bitch! Her own goddaughter, for Christ's sake, and you expect her to *believe* you?"

"Goddaughter?"

His face was close to mine now; hot beer breath touched my cheeks. "My ma's goddaughter was Ashley Heikkinen."

"That's impossible! I never had a godmother. I never met your mother until this afternoon."

The man shook his head. "I'll tell you what's impossible: Ashley Heikkinen appearing in Camel Rock after all these years. Ashley's dead. She died in a fire when she wasn't even two years old. My ma ought to know — she identified the body."

A chill washed over me from my scalp to my toes. The man stared, apparently recognizing my shock as genuine. After a moment I asked, "Where was the fire?"

He ignored the question, frowning. "Either you're a damned good actress or something weird's going on. Can't have been two people born with that name. Not in Camel Rock."

"Where was the fire?"

He shook his head again, this time as if to clear it. His mouth twisted, and I feared he was going to be sick. Then he let go of me and stumbled through the door to the parking lot. I released my breath in a long sigh and slumped against the wall. A car started outside. When its tires had spun on the gravel and its engine revved on the highway, I pushed myself upright and went along the hall to the empty lobby. A single bulb burned in the fixture above the reception desk, as it did every night. The usual sounds of laughter and conversation came from the tavern.

Everything seemed normal. Nothing was. I ran upstairs to the shelter of my room.

After I'd double-locked the door, I turned on the overhead and crossed to the bureau and leaned across it toward the streaky mirror. My face was drawn and unusually pale.

Ashley Heikkinen dead?

Dead in a fire when she wasn't quite two years old?

I closed my eyes, picturing the blackened ruin in the hills above town. Then I opened them and stared at my frightened face. It was the face of a stranger.

"If Ashley Heikkinen is dead," I said, "then who am *I*?"

Mrs. Fleming wouldn't talk to me. When I got to her cottage on one of the packed-dirt side streets at a little after nine the next morning, she refused to open the door and threatened to run me off with her dead husband's shotgun. "And don't think I'm not a good marksswoman," she added.

She must have gone straight to the phone, because Barbie was hanging up when I walked into the Beachcomber Shop a few minutes later. She frowned at me and said, "I just had the most insane call from Janet Fleming."

"About me?"

"How'd you guess? She was giving me all this stuff about you not being who you say you are and the 'real Ashley Heikkinen' dying in a fire when she was a baby. Must be going around the bend."

I sat down on the stool next to the counter. "Actually, there might be something to what she says." And then I told her all of it my mother's stories, the forbidden things that went unsaid, the burned-out cabin in the hills, my encounters with Janet Fleming and her son. "I tried to talk with Mrs. Fleming this morning," I finished, "But she threatened me with a shotgun."

102

"And she's been known to use that gun, too. You must've really upset her."

"Yes. From something she said yesterday afternoon, I gather she thinks I got hold of the other Ashley's birth certificate and created a set of fake ID around it."

"You sound like you believe there *was* another Ashley."

"I saw that burned-out cabin. Besides, why would Mrs. Fleming make something like that up?"

"But you recognized the cabin, both from my photograph and when you went there. You said it felt like home."

"I recognized it from my mother's stories, that's true. Barbie, I've lived those stories for most of my life. You know how kids sometimes get the notion that they're so special they can't really belong to their parents, that they're a prince or princess who was given to a servant couple to raise?"

"Oh sure, we all went through that stage. Only in my case, I was Mick Jagger's love child, and someday he was going to acknowledge me and give me all his money."

"Well, my mother's stories convinced me that I didn't really belong in a downscale tract in a crappy valley town. They made me special, somebody who came from a magical place. And I dreamed of it every night."

"So you're saying that you only recognized the cabin from the images your mother planted in your mind?"

"It's possible."

Barbie considered. "Okay, I'll buy that. And here's a scenario that might fit: After the fire, your parents moved away. That would explain why your mom didn't want to talk about why they left Camel Rock. And they had another child — you. They gave you Ashley's name and her history. It wasn't right, but grief does crazy things to otherwise sane people."

It worked — but only in part. "That still doesn't explain what happened to my father and why my mother would never talk about him."

"Maybe she was the one who went crazy with grief, and after a while he couldn't take it anymore, so he left."

She made it sound so logical and uncomplicated. But I'd known the quality of my mother's silences; there was more to them than Barbie's scenario encompassed.

I bit my lip in frustration. "You know, Mrs. Fleming could shed a lot of light on this, but she refuses to deal with me."

"Then find somebody who will."

"Who?" I asked. And then I thought of Gus Galick, the man Penny had told me about who had lived in Camel Rock all his life. "Barbie, do you know Gus Galick?"

"Sure. He's one of the few old-timers around here that I've really connected with. Gus builds ships in bottles; I sold some on consignment for him last year. He used to be a rumrunner during Prohibition, has some great stories about bringing in cases of Canadian booze to the coves along the coast."

"He must be older than God."

"Older than God and sharp as a tack. I bet he could tell you what you need to know."

"Penny said he was away on some charter trip."

"Was, but he's back now. I saw the *Irma* in her slip at the harbor when I drove by this morning."

Camel Rock's harbor was a sheltered cove with a bait shack and a few slips for fishing boats. Of them, Gus Galick's *Irma* was by far the most shipshape, and her captain was equally trim, with a shock of silvery-white hair and leathery tan skin. I didn't give him my name, just identified myself as a friend of Penny and Barbie. Galick seemed to take people at face value, though; he welcomed me on board, took me belowdecks, and poured me a cup of coffee in the cozy wood-paneled cabin. When we were seated on either side of the teak table, I asked my first question.

"Sure, I remember the fire on the old Carmichael estate," he said. "Summer of seventy-one. Both the father and the little girl died."

I gripped the coffee mug tighter. "The father died too?"

"Yeah. Heikkinen, his name was. Norwegian, maybe. I don't recall his first name, or the little girl's."

"John and Ashley."

"These people kin to you?"

"In a way. Mr. Galick, what happened to Melinda, the mother?"

He thought. "Left town, I guess. I never did see her after the double funeral."

"Where are John and Ashley buried?"

"Graveyard of the Catholic church." He motioned toward the hills, where I'd seen its spire protruding through the trees. "Carmichaels paid for everything, of course. Guilt, I guess."

"Why guilt?"

"The fire started on their land. Was the father's fault — John Heikkinen's, I mean — but still, they'd sacked him, and that was why he was drinking so heavy. Fell asleep with the doors to the woodstove open, and before he could wake up, the place was a furnace."

The free-flowing information was beginning to overwhelm me. "Let me get this straight: John Heikkinen worked for the Carmichaels?"

"Was their caretaker. His wife looked after their house."

"Where was she when the fire started?"

105

"At the main house, washing up the supper dishes. I heard she saw the flames, run down there, and tried to save her family. The Carmichaels held her back till the volunteer fire department could get there; they knew there wasn't any hope from the beginning."

I set the mug down, gripped the table's edge with icy fingers.

Galick leaned forward, eyes concerned. "Something wrong, miss? Have I upset you?"

I shook my head. "It's just . . . a shock, hearing about it after all these years." After a pause, I asked, "Did the Heikkinens have any other children?"

"Only the little girl who died."

I took out a photograph of my mother and passed it over to him. It wasn't a good picture, just a snap of her on the steps of our stucco bungalow down south. "Is this Melinda Heikkinen?"

He took a pair of glasses from a case on the table, put them on, and looked closely at it. Then he shrugged and handed it back to me. "There's some resemblance, but . . . She looks like she's had a hard life."

"She did." I replaced the photo in my wallet. "Can you think of anyone who could tell me more about the Heikkinens?"

"Well, there's Janet Fleming. She was Mrs. Heikkinen's aunt and the little girl's godmother. The mother was so broken up that Janet had to identify the bodies, so I guess she'd know everything there is to know about the fire."

"Anyone else?"

"Well, of course there's Madeline Carmichael. But she's living down at Timber Point now, and she never sees anybody."

"Why not?"

"I've got my ideas on that. It started after her husband died. Young man, only in his fifties. Heart attack." Galick grimaced. "Carmichael was one of these pillars of the community; never drank, smoked, or womanized. Keeled over at a church service in seventy-five. Me, I've lived a gaudy life, as they say. Even now I eat and drink all the wrong things, and I like a cigar after dinner. And I just go on and on. Tells you a lot about the randomness of it all."

I didn't want to think about that randomness; it was much too soon after losing my own mother to an untimely death for that. I asked, "About Mrs. Carmichael — it was her husband's death that turned her into a recluse?"

"No, miss." He shook his head firmly. "My idea is that his dying was just the last straw. The seeds were planted when their little girl disappeared three years before that."

"Disappeared?"

"It was in seventy-two, the year after the fire. The little girl was two years old, a change-of-life baby. Abigail, she was called. Abby, for short. Madeline Carmichael left her in her playpen on the veranda of their house, and she just plain vanished. At first they thought it was a kidnapping; the lumber company was failing, but the family still had plenty of money. But nobody ever made a ransom demand, and they never did find a trace of Abby or the person who took her."

The base of my spine began to tingle. As a child, I'd always been smaller than others of my age. Slower in school too. The way a child might be if she was a year younger than the age shown on her birth certificate.

Abigail Carmichael, I thought. Abby, for short.

The Catholic churchyard sat tucked back against a eucalyptus grove; the trees' leaves caught the sunlight in a subtle shimmer, and their aromatic buds were thick under my feet.

An iron fence surrounded the graves, and unpaved paths meandered among the mostly crumbling headstones. I meandered too, shock gradually leaching away to depression. The foundations of my life were as tilted as the oldest grave marker, and I wasn't sure I had the strength to construct new ones.

But I'd come here with a purpose, so finally I got a grip on myself and began covering the cemetery in a grid pattern.

I found them in the last row, where the fence backed up against the eucalyptus. Two small headstones set side by side. John and Ashley. There was room to John's right for another grave, one that now would never be occupied.

I knelt and brushed a curl of bark from Ashley's stone. The carving was simple, only her name and the dates. She'd been born April 6, 1969, and had died February 1, 1971.

I knelt there for a long time. Then I said goodbye and went home.

The old Carmichael house sat at the end of a chained-off drive that I'd earlier taken for a logging road. It was a wonder I hadn't stumbled across it in my search for the cabin. Built of dark timber and stone, with a wide veranda running the length of the lower story, it once might have been imposing. But now its windows were boarded, birds roosted in its eaves, and all around it the forest encroached. I followed a cracked flagstone path through a lawn long gone to weeds and wildflowers, to the broad front steps. Stood at their foot, my hand on the cold wrought-iron railing.

Could a child of two retain memories? I'd believed so before, but mine had turned out to be false, spoon-fed to me by the woman who had taken me from this veranda twenty-four years earlier. All the same, something in this lonely place spoke to me; I felt a sense of peace and safety that I'd never before experienced.

I hadn't known real security; my mother's and my life together had been too uncertain, too difficult, too shadowed by the past. Those circumstances probably accounted for my long string of failures, my inability to make my way in the world. A life built on lies and forbidden things was bound to go nowhere.

And yet it hadn't had to be that way. All this could have been mine, had it not been for a woman unhinged by grief. I could have grown up in this once lovely home, surrounded by my real parents' love. Perhaps if I had, my father would not have died of an untimely heart attack, and my birth mother would not have become a recluse. A sickening wave of anger swept over me, followed by a deep sadness. Tears came to my eyes, and I wiped them away.

I couldn't afford to waste time crying. Too much time had been wasted already.

To prove my real identity, I needed the help of Madeline Carmichael's attorney, and he took a good deal of convincing. I had to provide documentation and witnesses to my years as Ashley Heikkinen before he would consent to check Abigail Carmichael's birth records. Most of the summer went by before he broached the subject to Mrs. Carmichael. But blood composition and the delicate whorls on feet and fingers don't lie; finally, on a bright September afternoon, I arrived at Timber Point — alone, at the invitation of my birth mother.

I was nervous and gripped the Pinto's wheel with damp hands as I followed the guard's directions across a rolling seaside meadow to the Carmichael house. Like the others in this exclusive development, it was of modern design, with a silvery wood exterior that blended with the saw grass and Scotch broom. A glass wall faced the Pacific, reflecting sun glints on the water. Along the shoreline a flock of pelicans flew south in loose formation.

I'd worn my best dress — pink cotton, too light for the season, but it was all I had — and had spent a ridiculous amount of time on my hair and makeup. As I parked the shabby Pinto in the drive, I wished I could make it disappear. My approach to the door was awkward; I stumbled on the unlandscaped ground and almost turned my ankle. The uniformed maid who admitted me gave me the kind of glance that once, as a hostess at a coffee shop, I'd reserved for customers without shirt or shoes. She showed me to a living room facing the sea and went away.

I stood in the room's center on an Oriental carpet, unsure whether to sit or stand. Three framed photographs on a grand piano caught my attention; I went over there and looked at them. A man and a woman, middle-aged and handsome. A child, perhaps a year old, in a striped romper. The child had my eyes.

"Yes, that's Abigail." The throaty voice — smoker's voice — came from behind me. I turned to face the woman in the photograph. Older now, but still handsome, with upswept creamy white hair and pale porcelain skin, she wore a long caftan in some sort of soft champagne-colored fabric. No reason for Madeline Carmichael to get dressed; she never left the house.

She came over to me and peered at my face. For a moment her eyes were soft and questioning, then they hardened and looked away. "Please," she said, "sit down over here."

I followed her to two matching brocade settees positioned at right angles to the seaward window. We sat, one on each, with a coffee table between us. Mrs. Carmichael took a cigarette from a silver box on the table and lit it with a matching lighter.

Exhaling and fanning the smoke away, she said, "I have a number of things to say to you that will explain my position in this matter. First, I believe the evidence you've presented. You are my daughter Abigail. Melinda Heikkinen was very bitter toward my husband and me: If we hadn't dismissed her husband, he wouldn't have been passed out from drinking when the fire started. If we hadn't kept her late at her duties that night, she would have been home and able to prevent it. If we hadn't stopped her from plunging into the conflagration, she might have saved her child. That, I suppose, served to justify her taking our child as a replacement."

She paused to smoke. I waited.

"The logic of what happened seems apparent at this remove," Mrs. Carmichael added, "but at the time we didn't think to mention Melinda as a potential suspect. She'd left Camel Rock the year before; even her aunt, Janet Fleming, had heard nothing from her. My husband and I had more or less put her out of our minds. And of course, neither of us was thinking logically at the time."

I was beginning to feel uneasy. She was speaking so analytically and dispassionately — not at all like a mother who had been reunited with her long-lost child.

She went on: "I must tell you about our family. California pioneers on both sides. The Carmichaels were lumber barons. My family were merchant princes engaging in the China trade. Abigail was the last of both lines, born to carry on our tradition. Surely you can understand why this matter is so . . . difficult."

She was speaking of Abigail as someone separate from me. "What matter?" I asked.

"That role in life, the one Abigail was born to, takes a certain type of individual. My Abby, the child I would have raised had it not been for Melinda Heikkinen, would not have turned out so —" She bit her lower lip, looked away at the sea.

"So what, Mrs. Carmichael?"

She shook her head, crushing out her cigarette.

A wave of humiliation swept over me. I glanced down at my cheap pink dress, at a chip in the polish on my thumbnail. When I raised my eyes, my birth mother was examining me with faint distaste.

I'd always had a temper; now it rose, and I gave in to it. "So *what*, Mrs. Carmichael?" I repeated. "So *common?*"

She winced but didn't reply.

I said, "I suppose you think it's your right to judge a person on her appearance or her financial situation. But you should remember that my life hasn't been easy — not like yours. Melinda Heikkinen could never make ends meet. We lived in a valley town east of L.A. She was sick a lot. I had to work from the time I was fourteen. There was trouble with gangs in our neighborhood."

Then I paused, hearing myself. No, I would not do this. I would not whine or beg.

"I wasn't brought up to complain," I continued, "and I'm not complaining now. In spite of working, I graduated high school with honors. I got a small scholarship, and Melinda persuaded me to go to college. She helped out financially when she could. I didn't finish, but that was my own fault. Whatever mistakes I've made are my own doing, not Melinda's. Maybe she told me lies about our life here on the coast, but they gave me something to hang on to. A lot of the time they were all I had, and now they've been taken from me. But I'm still not complaining."

Madeline Carmichael's dispassionate facade cracked. She closed her eyes, compressed her lips. After a moment she said, "How can you defend that woman?"

"For twenty-four years she was the only mother I knew."

Her eyes remained closed. She said, "Please, I will pay you any amount of money if you will go away and pretend this meeting never took place."

For a moment I couldn't speak. Then I exclaimed, "I don't want your money! This is not about money!"

"What, then?"

"What do I want? I thought I wanted my real mother."

"And now that you've met me, you're not sure you do." She opened her eyes, looked directly into mine. "Our feelings aren't really all that different, are they, Abigail?"

I shook my head in confusion.

Madeline Carmichael took a deep breath. "Abigail, you say you lived on Melinda's lies, that they were something to sustain you?"

I nodded.

"I've lived on lies too, and they sustained *me*. For twenty-three years I've put myself to sleep with dreams of our meeting. I woke to them. No matter what I was doing, they were only a fingertip's reach away. And now they've been taken from me, as yours have. My Abby, the daughter I pictured in those dreams, will never walk into this room and make everything all right. Just as the things you've dreamed of are never going to happen."

I looked around the room — at the grand piano, the Oriental carpets, the antiques and exquisite art objects. Noticed for the first time how stylized and sterile it was, how

113

the cold expanse of glass beside me made the sea blinding and bleak.

"You're right," I said, standing up. "Even if you were to take me in and offer me all this, it wouldn't be the life I wanted."

Mrs. Carmichael extended a staying hand toward me.

I stepped back. "No. And don't worry — I won't bother you again."

As I went out into the quicksilver afternoon and shut the door behind me, I thought that even though Melinda Heikkinen had given me a difficult life, she'd also offered me dreams to soften the hard times and love to ease my passage. My birth mother hadn't even offered me coffee or tea.

On a cold, rainy December evening, Barbie Cannon and I sat at a table near the fireplace in the hotel's tavern, drinking red wine in celebration of my good fortune.

"I can't believe," she said for what must have been the dozenth time, "that old lady Carmichael up and gave you her house in the hills."

"Any more than you can believe I accepted it."

"Well, I thought you were too proud to take her money."

"Too proud to be bought off, but she offered the house with no strings attached. Besides, it's in such bad shape that I'll probably be fixing it up for the rest of my life."

"And she probably took a big tax write-off on it. No wonder rich people stay rich." Barbie snorted. "By the way, how come you're still calling yourself Ashley Heikkinen?"

I shrugged. "Why not? It's been my name for as long as I can remember. It's a good name."

"You're acting awfully laid back about this whole thing."

"You didn't see me when I got back from Timber Point. But I've worked it all through. In a way, I understand how

Mrs. Carmichael feels. The house is nice, but anything else she could have given me isn't what I was looking for."

"So what *were* you looking for?"

I stared into the fire. Madeline Carmichael's porcelain face flashed against the background of the flames. Instead of anger I felt a tug of pity for her: a lonely woman waiting her life out, but really as dead and gone as the merchant princes, the lumber barons, the old days on this wild north coast. Then I banished the image and pictured instead the faces of the friends I'd made since coming to Camel Rock: Barbie, Penny and Gene, the couple who ran the herb farm, Gus Galick, and — now — Janet Fleming and her son, Stu. Remembered all the good times: dinners and walks on the beach, Penny and Gene's fortieth wedding anniversary party, Barbie's first photographic exhibit, a fishing trip on Gus's trawler. And thought of all the good times to come.

"What was I looking for?" I said. "Something I found the day I got here."

Part II:

Stories by
Marcia Muller
and
Bill Pronzini

Cache and Carry

(A Sharon McCone/"Nameless Detective" Story)

"Hello?"

"Wolf? It's Sharon McCone."

"Well! Been a while, Sharon. How are you?"

"I've been better. Are you busy?"

"No, no, I just got home. What's up?"

"I've got a problem and I thought you might be able to help."

"If I can. Professional problem?"

"The kind you've run into before."

"Oh?"

"One of those things that *seem* impossible but that you know has to have a simple explanation."

". . . ."

"Wolf, are you there?"

"I'm here. The poor man's Sir Henry Merrivale."

"Who's Sir Henry Merrivale?"

"Never mind. Tell me your tale of woe."

"Well, one of All Souls's clients is a small outfit in the Outer Mission called Neighborhood Check Cashing. You know, one of these places that cashes third-party or social-security checks for local residents who don't have bank accounts of their own or easy access to a bank. We did some legal work for them a year or so ago, when they first opened for business."

"Somebody rip them off?"

"Yes. For two thousand dollars."

"Uh-huh. When?"

"Sometime this morning."

"Why did you and All Souls get called in on a police matter?"

"The police were called first but they couldn't come up with any answers. So Jack Harvey, Neighborhood's owner and manager, contacted me. But I haven't come up with any answers either."

"Go ahead. I'm listening."

"There's no way anyone could have gotten the two thousand dollars out of Neighborhood's office. And yet, if the money is still hidden somewhere on the premises, the police couldn't find it and neither could I."

"Mmm."

"Only one of two people could have taken it — unless Jack Harvey himself is responsible, and I don't believe that. If I knew which one, I might have an idea of what happened to the money. Or vice versa. But I don't have a clue either way."

"Let's have the details."

"Well, cash is delivered twice a week — Mondays and Thursdays — by armored car at the start of the day's business. It's usually five thousand dollars, unless Jack requests more or less. Today it was exactly five thousand."

"Not a big operation, then."

"No. Jack's also an independent insurance broker; the employees help him out in that end of the business too."

"His employees are the two who could have stolen the money?"

"Yes. Art DeWitt, the bookkeeper, and Maria Chavez, the cashier. DeWitt's twenty-five, single, lives in Daly City.

120

He's studying business administration nights at City College. Chavez is nineteen, lives with her family in the Mission. She's planning to get married next summer. They both seem to check out as solid citizens."

"But you say one of them has to be guilty. Why?"

"Opportunity. Let me tell you what happened this morning. The cash was delivered as usual, and Maria Chavez entered the amount in her daily journal, then put half the money in the till and half in the safe. Business for the first hour and a half was light; only one person came in to cash a small check: Jack Harvey's cousin, whom he vouches for."

"So Chavez couldn't have passed the money to him or another accomplice."

"No. At about ten-thirty a local realtor showed up wanting to cash a fairly large check: thirty-five hundred dollars. Harvey usually doesn't like to do that, because Neighborhood runs short before the next cash delivery. Besides, the fee for cashing a large check is the same as for a small one; he stands to lose on large transactions. But the realtor is a good friend, so he okayed it. When Chavez went in to cash the check, there was only five hundred dollars in the till."

"Did DeWitt also have access to the till?"

"Yes."

"Any way either of them could have slipped out of the office for even a few seconds?"

"No. Harvey's desk is by the back door and he was sitting there the entire time."

"What about through the front?"

"The office is separated from the customer area by one of those double Plexiglass security partitions and a locked security door. The door operates by means of a buzzer at

Harvey's desk. He didn't buzz anybody in or out."

"Could the two thousand have been removed between the time the police searched and you were called in?"

"No way. When the police couldn't find it in the office, they body-searched DeWitt and had a matron do the same with Chavez. The money wasn't on either of the them. Then, after the cops left, Jack told his employees they couldn't take anything away from the office except Chavez's purse and DeWitt's briefcase, both of which he searched again, personally."

"Do either DeWitt or Chavez have a key to the office?"

"No."

"Which means the missing money is still there."

"Evidently. But *where*, Wolf?"

"Describe the office to me."

"One room, with an attached lavatory that doubles as a supply closet. Table, with a desktop copier, postage scale, postage meter. A big Mosler safe; only Harvey has the combination. Three desks: Jack's next to the back door; DeWitt's in the middle; Chavez's next to the counter behind the partition, where the till is. Desks have standard stuff on them — adding machines, a typewriter on Chavez's, family photos, stack trays, staplers, pen sets. Everything you'd expect to find."

"Anything you *wouldn't* expect to find?"

"Not unless you count some lurid romance novels that Chavez likes to read on her lunch break."

"Did anything unusual happen this morning, before the shortage was discovered?"

"Not really. The toilet backed up and ruined a bunch of supplies, but Jack says that's happened three or four times before. Old plumbing."

"Uh-huh."

"You see why I'm frustrated? There just doesn't seem to be any clever hidey-hole in that office. And Harvey's already started to tear his hair. Chavez and DeWitt resent the atmosphere of suspicion; they're nervous, too, and have both threatened to quit. Harvey doesn't want to lose the one that isn't guilty, anymore than he wants to lose his two thousand dollars."

"How extensive was the search you and the police made?"

"About as extensive as you can get."

"Desks gone over from top to bottom, drawers taken out?"

"Yes."

"Underside of the legs checked?"

"Yes."

"Same thing with all the chairs?"

"To the point of removing cushions and seat backs."

"The toilet backing up — any chance that could be connected?"

"I don't see how. Harvey and I both looked it over pretty carefully. The sink and the rest of the plumbing, too."

"What about the toilet paper roll?"

"I checked it. Negative."

"Chavez's romance novels — between the pages?"

"I thought of that. Negative."

"Personal belongings?"

"All negative. Including Jack Harvey's. I went through his on the idea that DeWitt or Chavez might have thought to use him as a carrier."

"The office equipment?"

"Checked and rechecked. Copier, negative. Chavez's typewriter, negative. Postage meter and scale, negative. Four adding machines, negative. Stack trays —"

"Wait a minute, Sharon. *Four* adding machines?"

"That's right."

"Why four, with only three people?"

"DeWitt's office machine jammed and he had to bring his own from home."

"When did that happen?"

"It jammed two days ago. He brought his own yesterday."

"Suspicious coincidence, don't you think?"

"I did at first. But I checked both machines, inside and out. Negative."

"Did either DeWitt or Chavez bring anything else to the office in recent days that they haven't brought before?"

"Jack says no."

"Then we're back to DeWitt's home adding machine."

"Wolf, I told you —"

"What kind is it? Computer type, or the old-fashioned kind that runs a tape"

"The old-fashioned kind."

"Did you run a tape on it? Or on the office machine that's supposed to be jammed?"

". . . No. No, I didn't."

"Maybe you should. Both machines are still in the office, right?"

"Yes."

"Why don't you have another look at them? Run tapes on both, see if the office model really is jammed — or if maybe it's DeWitt's home model that doesn't work the way it should."

"And if it's the home model, have it taken apart piece by piece."

"Right."

"I'll call Harvey and have him meet me at Neighborhood right away."

"Let me know, huh? Either way?"

"You bet I will."

"Wolf, hi. It's Sharon."

"You sound chipper. Good news?"

"Yes, thanks to you. You were right about the adding machines. I ran a tape on DeWitt's office model and it worked fine. But the one he brought from home didn't, for a damned good reason."

"Which is?"

"Its tape roll was a dummy. Hollow, made of metal and wood with just enough paper tape to make it look like the real thing. So real neither the police nor I thought to remove and examine it before. The missing money was inside."

"So DeWitt must have been planning the theft for some time."

"That's what he confessed to the police a few minutes ago. He made the dummy roll in his workshop at home; took him a couple of weeks. It was in his home machine when he brought that in yesterday. This morning he slipped the roll out and put it into his pocket. When Maria Chavez was in the lavatory and Jack Harvey was occupied on the phone, he lifted the money from the till and pocketed that too. He went into the john after Marie came out and hid the money in the dummy roll. Then, back at his desk, he put the fake roll into his own machine, which he intended to take home with him this evening. It was his bad luck — and Jack's good luck — that the realtor came in with such a large check to cash."

"I suppose he intended to doctor the books to cover the theft."

"So he said. You know, Wolf, it's too bad DeWitt didn't

apply his creative talents to some legitimate enterprise. His cache-and-carry scheme was really pretty clever."

"What kind of scheme?"

"Cache and carry. C-a-c-h-e."

". . . ."

"Was that a groan I heard?"

"McCone, if you're turning into a rogue detective, call somebody else next time you come up against an impossible problem. Call Sir Henry Merrivale."

"What do you mean, a rogue detective?"

"The worse kind there is. A punslinger."

The Dying Time

MELISSA

Autumn leaves skittered along the narrow main street of the small town in California's Gold Country. They leapt the high curb, rattled down the board sidewalk, and drifted against the bench where I sat dying.

Was this where it was to end — Murphys, population around three hundred? A hard, wooden-slatted bench my last resting place in this life? Tricked-up shops and polyester-clad tourists my last sight? What was I doing here, anyway? Traveling aimlessly, as my husband and I had done over the past five years, possessed of more time and money than purposes and enthusiasms.

The pain was growing stronger now; if I had any chance to survive I had better do something soon. But I felt curiously lethargic and resigned. Even the prospect of a painful death didn't seem to bother me.

It had been a good life up until this past year. I'd accomplished most of the modest things I'd set out to do, had visited most of the places I wanted to see. Of course there were loose ends, but didn't everyone leave a few of those? There was the emptiness of the past few years, but what were a few out of many? And then there were the events of September and my growing suspicions about the terrible way Jake Hollis had died. . . .

I didn't want to think about Jake. That was in the past, over now. All over. As my life soon would be.

Strange. I hadn't expected to feel such detachment at the end. I seemed as little a part of the dying woman on the bench as the leaves that drifted at her feet. They were dying too, torn by the wind from the trees that had sustained them through the sudden rainstorms of spring, the blistering heat of summer, the first frosts of autumn. Dying like —

"What the hell's the matter with you?"

Slowly I looked up. My husband Ray, returned from the used bookshop with a package under his arm. A handsome man yet, blond and tanned and fit, dressed in a new brown cashmere sweater and cords. Handsome as the day I'd met him at the sorority open house twenty-six years ago. A quarter-century of marriage, so long that I could scarcely remember a time when he wasn't there. Always there, yet so often absent even when physically present.

I should have sensed that quality even before we were married. The way his eyes kept moving restlessly as he pretended interest in what I was saying. The way he replied with nods and utterances that were mere reaction to my tone of voice, rather than my words' content. But I was twenty years old; what did I know of a man for whom the real world was never quite enough? A man who sought elusive fulfillment in the new and strange and different, as if he might then enter another dimension that would measure up to his expectations.

Nothing had ever measured up. Nothing. Not a stellar career that began with the glimmerings of what the media now called the Information Age and culminated with the sale of the last of three computer firms he'd founded — a sale unprecedented in financial annals that insured the security of our children and their heirs for generations to come. The children — Donna and Andrew — certainly hadn't measured up; he'd given them scant attention, and

128

now they had drifted away. There were the various pursuits, all dangerous — flying, mountain climbing, auto racing — and now all discarded. Even the latest passion, skydiving, was a thing of the past. I would be the last to go, the wife who had become nothing more than a good traveling companion.

The Caribbean in winter, when rains soaked northern California. Paris in the springtime. Alaskan cruises to escape the heat of summer in the Napa Valley. African photo safaris, visits to Egypt's pyramids, tours of China and Russia. Hawaii at the holidays when our children and their families failed to return home. We migrated like birds, but insulated from unpleasantness and with fewer surprises.

Until this past month —

"Melissa, I asked you, what's the matter?" Feigned concern turned the fine lines at his eyes' corners to furrows.

With an effort I said, "I'm not feeling well."

"I told you you shouldn't have made that chicken pasta for lunch. It's a warm day, and heavy food and wine —"

I nodded wearily. It wasn't the pasta or the wine, but there was no point in arguing. The only point was in calling for help, trying to save myself. And I still couldn't seem to care.

I was dying, and Ray had poisoned me.

RAY

Melissa didn't want to leave the bench. "It's already too late, isn't it?" she said dully.

"Too late for what?"

"Oh God, Ray, I can die here as well as anywhere else. It's peaceful here —"

"Die? Don't be silly, you're not going to die."

129

She squeezed her eyes shut, grimacing, and wouldn't say another word.

I was tempted to let her sit there with her stomach ache and suffer. She could be exasperating sometimes, when she was in one of her moods. She tended to exaggerate and overdramatize situations even at her best, and whenever she was hurt or upset or angry, she retreated so deeply inside herself that no matter what I did or how hard I tried, I couldn't reach her.

Not that I'd ever been able to get to the core of her, really, except in small ways and for short glimpses. There was just no common ground for us. I live in the real world; I don't believe in anything I can't touch or see or smell. I have strong appetites — sex, food, danger. I take life in both hands and squeeze hard. Melissa is just the opposite. She's a romantic, a sentimentalist; she lives in a fantasy world of dreams and ideals, searching for comforts and fulfillments that I can't give her, nobody can give her, because even she doesn't understand exactly what it is she wants out of life. Little-girl-lost is an apt description of her. Dorothy wandering around in some fantastic Oz of her own devising, where everything and everybody is strange and bewildering.

That lost quality was part of what attracted me to her in the beginning. It's very appealing in a beautiful young woman; it makes her more desirable, the chase and catch more exhilarating. Chase and catch weren't enough for me in Melissa's case, though. Before we slept together the first time I knew I was in love with her. But how can you keep on loving someone you can touch only part of the time, like a ghost who drifts in and out of your life and bed, substantial for a while and then little more than vapor? I don't deal well with frustration or failure, yet that's what Melissa had come to represent.

130

It was the same for her, I suppose. I'm not what she wants or understands, either. That's why she keeps drifting from one affair to another — looking for someone who's more like she is, who can give her what she wants or thinks she wants. A satisfaction I could always take until recently is that none of the men measured up any more than I have. None until the last one.

Jake Hollis. My good sky-diving pal Jake.

He must have measured up. He must've been what she wanted. Otherwise, why would the two of them have plotted to kill me?

She had to have been part of it, much as I hated the thought. It'd been her idea that Jake and I go jumping that day; I remember her suggesting it. And she'd gone along with us, the first time in years she wanted to be in the plane for one of my dives. I don't know why I agreed. I knew by then she was sleeping with Hollis. But murder . . . the possibility never even occurred to me.

His hands on my back, clawing at my chute . . . I can still feel them. Trying to rip the pack off so I'd plummet to my death. A few years younger, a little stronger, but not as determined to survive as I'd been. That's the main reason his chute was the one damaged in the struggle, his body the one that plummeted two thousand feet to shatter on the hard earth.

She didn't cry for him, at least not in front of me. Shock, horror, but no tears. Retreated inside herself to that place no one else can ever go — like the Cheshire Cat when it vanished. If she had cried in front of me, I think I would've confronted her then and there. Two weeks now since it happened and I still haven't done it. And I don't know why. This trip to the Sierra foothills, the pretense that everything is reasonably normal between us . . . it's a fool's game. If she and one of her lovers had tried to kill me in the past, I wouldn't have hesitated in accusing her, throwing her out, taking some sort of revenge. Now . . . I don't know. I'm still hanging onto life with both hands, but the grip isn't as strong as it used to be. Neither are the highs or the lows, the emotions that once raged in me like torrents. It's as if part of me, or something within me, did die that day, along with Jake Hollis.

I ought to hate her, but I don't.

I feel sorry for her.

She was still sitting with her eyes closed, her hands clutched at her middle, her mouth twisted. Typical of her. An upset stomach, and she turns it into high drama.

"Melissa," I said, "we're going back to the lodge. Right now."

She didn't object this time. "All right."

I helped her up, put my arm around her and led her to the car. People watched us, one or two with concerned expressions or small approving smiles. Solicitous husband helping unwell wife. The scene was so outwardly caring, loving that I felt an urge to laugh. But I didn't. There was nothing left to laugh about.

And now *my* stomach was beginning to bother me. Sharp little cramping pains. Sympathy pains? That was almost funny too — but not quite.

I helped Melissa into the car and took us away from the watching eyes, away from Murphys. Tom Moore's hunting lodge was eight miles higher up in the mountains — a secluded retreat, a place for lovers. Why had I agreed to come here? Why had Melissa agreed? What was the sense in us getting away alone together, with the end for us so near?

Halfway to the lodge, the cramps grew worse. The pain

was stabbing and I was feeling nauseous by the time I reached the turnoff.

Beside me, Melissa sat hunched over, holding her stomach, her face pale. Pretending, to throw me off guard? Those thoughts came on the heels of the other one, the one that made me jerk and clench my hands tight around the wheel.

Christ, what if she'd poisoned me?

MELISSA

In the car on the road leading to our borrowed mountain cabin Ray asked me in what way I wasn't feeling well. Nausea and stomach cramps, I told him, as well as a headache.

"Must be the flu," he said. "I feel the same way, except I've also got chills."

Liar, I thought. This was like no flu I'd ever experienced. "How long have you felt sick?"

"A little while."

Then why had he eaten with apparent enjoyment a huge helping of the chicken pasta I'd fixed for lunch? Why had he suggested we drive into town and then spent so long browsing in the bookshop if he was feeling bad? Faking, of course, so I wouldn't guess the truth. Except that I'd already guessed it.

"How awful for you," I said.

"You're certainly the sympathetic one."

I turned my face to the side window and didn't reply. My cramps were growing worse; the poison was doing its work.

At the rustic wood-and-stone lodge belonging to Tom Moore, his former business partner, Ray pulled the car close to the front steps, jumped out, and rushed up them without waiting for me. By the time I made my way inside he was in the bathroom off the front hallway, making violent retching sounds. Acting again.

He was a consummate actor, I thought as I went upstairs to the living room and slumped in one of the armchairs in front of the huge fireplace. All those years of high-level business dealings, all those years of pretending interest in and affection for the children and me — they had polished his art. And now he was playing his biggest role of all, unaware that his audience of one wasn't the slightest bit fooled.

I leaned my head back against the chair, narrowed my eyes, and looked around. Knotty pine everywhere. God, how I hated knotty pine! Every uncomfortable mountain or lakefront cabin I'd ever stayed in was paneled in the stuff, and now I was going to die surrounded by it.

A violent surge of nausea swept through me; bile rose in my throat. Ray was still in the downstairs bathroom, and I'd never make it upstairs in time, so I rushed to the kitchen and was sick in the sink. Leaning with my hands braced against the countertop, I thought distractedly, All the work I did cleaning up in here — ruined. Not that Tim would care. The man's become a slob since his poor wife died.

His poor wife died . . .

That's what they'd be saying about Ray soon. What did he plan to tell people? That I'd been poisoned by accident? Or did he intend to get rid of my body? Claim I'd disappeared? Bury me someplace in these woods . . . ?

My stomach contracted again; another cramp, more intense than any pain I'd ever experienced outside of childbirth, left me weak and breathless. And suddenly the apathy I'd felt since Murphys was gone. I *didn't* want to die this way, in agony. I didn't want to die at all. I'd thought I already had, spiritually, as I watched Jake Hollis plummet through the air. But that simply wasn't true.

After a moment I felt well enough to move across the room to a little desk with shelves containing cookbooks and other household volumes. The chills Ray had mentioned were starting now. What kind of poison produced chills? Had Ray chosen it because its symptoms mimicked a bad case of the flu? He hadn't wanted me to know I was dying.

Unlike Jake. *He'd* known in those last few awful minutes.

The scene I'd witnessed from the plane two weeks earlier replayed itself in my mind: Ray and Jake struggling in mid air, neither chute open. Ray's suddenly blossoming upward, while Jake fell, arms and legs flailing. And when the pilot and I arrived at the airstrip, there was Ray, pretending to be completely broken up over our friend's death. Over and over he repeated, "I just don't know what happened."

And I had kept my silence, even though I knew what had happened — and why.

Jake Hollis was dead. Perhaps the closest person to a friend Ray ever had. My friend too; I'd turned to him in desperation when I sensed my marriage was finally about to end. Not for sex, as I had to two other men in the past, but for insight into what had brought Ray and me to this point. But although Jake had heard me out through two long lunches and an afternoon of drinks, he could shed no light on the situation. Ray had kept him at as much of an arm's length as he had me.

For days after Jake's death I'd felt numb, unable to cry, unable to confront Ray with the fact that I knew what he'd done. I even tried to deny it myself, pretend I hadn't seen the mid air struggle; it seemed too monstrous an act for the man I'd lived with for a quarter of a century. But then a violent scene from five years before escaped from where I'd buried it in my memory: Ray raging at me, having found out about the second of my two brief affairs. His face red and

135

contorted, his eyes wild, he'd accused me of repeated infi-
delities throughout our marriage. Berated me for sleeping
with a member of his mountain-climbing team. Screamed,
"I'll kill him! I swear, on the next climb I'll grab hold of
him and pitch him off Denali! If I have to go down with
him, I will!"

He hadn't, of course. Instead he'd spent five years nurs-
ing his rage and imagining I was sleeping with every man I
met. And when that rage was at a fever pitch, he'd turned it
on Jake. Killed his friend because he overheard a phone call
between us. Killed him because another so-called friend
had told him of seeing Jake and me in intimate conversation
in a neighborhood cocktail lounge. I'd denied either when
he asked me about them; now I wished I had told him why
I'd been talking to Jake.

I lay my aching head on the desk and moaned. Finally
the tears that shock had frozen began to flow.

Why did you kill him, Ray?

Why didn't you just kill me?

RAY

Emptying my stomach didn't help much. I still felt sick and
shaky when I came out of the downstairs bathroom. This
wasn't the flu or any other kind of natural illness; there was no
doubt of it now. Call 911, I thought, ask for medical assistance. But it would take awhile for an ambulance or med-evac
helicopter to get here from Jackson or Sonora and I could be
dead by then.

What kind of poison had she used? If I knew that, there
might be something I could take to counteract it. At least I
could tell the emergency operator, who could then alert the
paramedics.

It was an effort to climb the stairs to the upper floor. Ray

136

Porter, who had climbed mountains, hiked through jungles and across deserts — so damn weak he couldn't mount a dozen steps without streaming sweat and hanging onto the railing with both hands. It enraged me, the idea of dying this way, weak and helpless. Yet the funny thing was, most of the rage was at myself for allowing such a thing to happen.

My fault, as much as Melissa's. I'd driven her into Jake Hollis's arms, the arms of all the others. I'd destroyed her, slowly and surely, with the heat of my passions. And in the process I'd sown the seeds of my own destruction.

But not blaming her or hating her didn't mean I would let her get away with what she'd done. Life was still precious to me, and I wouldn't let go of it without a fight.

She wasn't in the kitchen. She had been, though; as I passed the stove I smelled a sour odor and saw that she'd thrown up in the sink. My God! Maybe she hadn't been faking in Murphys or on the way up here; maybe she'd poisoned herself too. Hollis was dead, she couldn't have him, and she didn't want me any more, so what did she have left to live for? It was just like her to concoct a quixotic Shakespearean finish for both of us.

I stumbled into the living room. She wasn't there, either, but I could hear her — low sobbing sounds coming from out on the balcony that ran across the entire rear of the lodge. I almost fell before I reached the open balcony doors; I had to clutch at the glass for support, all but drag myself around the jamb. The weakness and the cramping pain made me even more determined.

Melissa was sitting on one of the redwood chairs, her arms wrapped across her middle, rocking slightly and grimacing. A closed book lay in her lap. A *book*, for God's sake, at a time like this!

"Melissa."

137

She stiffened and her head turned toward me. Her eyes were enormous, luminous with pain. In spite of what she'd done, in spite of myself, I experienced a surge of feeling for her — compassion, protectiveness, even tenderness, like suddenly materialized ghosts from the past.

"Why, Ray?" she said. "Why did this have to happen?"

"You know the answer to that better than I do. But it's not too late. I won't let it be too late."

"I don't want to die. I thought I did, for a while, but I don't."

"Neither of us is going to die. I'll call for emergency medical help . . . but I have to know what it was first."

She shook her head as if she didn't understand.

"The poison," I said. "What kind of poison?"

"How should I know! Ray, don't torture me any more —"

"Listen to me. It's not too late. An antidote, some kind of emetic . . . what did you use?"

"I didn't . . . I didn't . . ."

I lurched toward her, fell to my knees beside her chair. "How long ago? What kind of poison? How much?"

"Stop it! You know it wasn't me!"

"Melissa —"

"*You* did it. You, you, you!"

I stared at her in disbelief. "That's crazy. I wouldn't do a thing like that to you, to myself. I wouldn't hurt you."

"But if you didn't poison us . . ."

"I didn't." Confusion gripped me now; I couldn't seem to think clearly. "And you swear you didn't?"

"I swear!"

"If it wasn't poison, then what —" I broke off, staring at the book in her lap, seeing its title for the first time. *Symptoms: The Complete Home Medical Encyclopedia.*

I reached out to it — and the pain came again, a sudden wrenching so violent it brought an involuntary cry out of my throat. Gagging, I clutched at Melissa. Felt her hands on me. And then we were clinging to each other, holding tight, tighter than we had in a long, long time.

MELISSA

As Ray knelt beside my chair and we held each other, I felt something that I'd never felt for him before: compassion. He'd never needed it, never wanted it, and he probably wouldn't now. But a man who had climbed mountains, who had been unafraid to step out into space with only a parachute to depend on — It tore at my heart to see him reduced to this sweating, trembling weakness by . . . what?

He was staring at the home medical encyclopedia that I'd found on the shelf above the kitchen desk. Now he raised his eyes to mine and said thickly, "Did you look up our symptoms in there?"

"No, not yet . . ."

He reached again for the book, but another wave of pain drove him down into a sitting position, forehead against my knees.

"Can't do it," he said. "My eyes . . ."

The admission seemed to rob him of his last strength. Ray had always taken charge; always, in every situation.

A sharp spasm wrenched my stomach. When it eased, I put my hand on the back of his head and said, "I can."

It was a huge volume, and for a moment I couldn't focus on how to use it. Then I realized the first part was a reverse dictionary of symptoms; you looked yours up, and it referred you to the causes described in the second section. I started with the section on nausea and vomiting.

"This doesn't help," I muttered after scanning the entry.

Vomiting . . . 'Characteristic of nearly all infectious diseases,' none of which it was likely we'd both come down with . . . Wait, here was vomiting coupled with headache. . . .

Ray grabbed onto my calves now, his fingers spasming along with his body. More cramps, worse than what I was experiencing. I gripped his shoulder reassuringly and read on.

Brain tumors, migraine headache, acute glaucoma . . .

Oh, God, this was no good! I felt the beginnings of panic, took a deep breath and continued skimming the entry. It told me nothing.

Ray moaned, his face contorted.

I flipped to the front of the book, looking for a table of contents. An encyclopedia of symptoms — wouldn't they expect that a user might be in pain, want answers in a hurry? Why wasn't there —

Severe pain in the abdomen, nausea, cramps, vomiting.

Acute gastritis . . . Staphlococcus . . . Botulism . . .

"I've narrowed it down. Hold on."

"What . . . ?"

A strong spasm stiffened me before I could focus clearly on the next page. The chills that followed were intense enough to make my teeth chatter.

"Melissa?"

"I'll be all right in a minute. Are your eyes any better?"

"A little." He fumbled the book toward him.

"Look at page three fifty-two, darling. Three fifty-two. . . ."

RAY

Darling. Had I heard that right? She hadn't called me darling, dear, honey, any of the endearments in a long while, even on the rare occasions the past few years when we'd made love . . .

Another twinge of pain made me grit my teeth, focus on the open book. Page 352. Infected Food, Gastroenteritis. Usually due to eating food that is infected by salmonella bacteria.

Food poisoning. What fools we'd been, each imagining that the other had resorted to arsenic, strychnine, some damn thing. And all along —

"Salmonella," I said. "But how did we get it? We haven't eaten anywhere but here the past couple of days."

"The kitchen! You remember how filthy it was when we arrived? I thought I cleaned everything thoroughly, but I must've missed something . . . That damn plastic cutting board. Bacteria breeds in plastic like that, and I diced the raw chicken on it for our pasta."

Rarely fatal, the book said. But nevertheless a Medical Alert. Severe cases develop dehydration, kidney failure with urinary suppression, shock. Call physician immediately.

"Nine-eleven," I said. "Can't waste any more time." I tried to push up onto my feet, but I seemed to have no strength in my arms or legs. The entire lower half of my body felt heavy, almost numb from the vomiting and cramping.

"You're too weak."

"No. I've got to make the call . . ."

"You ate more than I did," Melissa said, "your case is more severe. I feel better now — I'll do it." She touched my face. "I'm the strong one right now, darling. Let me be the strong one for once."

I looked up at her through the wetness and the pain. The same Melissa, the same woman I'd married and had children with and lived with for a quarter of a century. And yet she seemed different somehow. Or maybe I was seeing her differently. The little-girl-lost quality was gone; for the first time I saw strength in my wife. Hazily I wondered if it were something new, a courage born of this crisis, or if it had been there all along, hidden or suppressed or just not visible to me for what it was.

I clung to the chair, weak, and watched Melissa stand up, strong, and make her way toward the open doors. And a voice that didn't sound like mine, that almost whimpered like a hurt child's, called after her, "Hurry, baby, hurry . . ."

MELISSA

Ray had collapsed against the chair when I came back. "They're sending a med-evac helicopter," I told him. "We're going to be okay." Then I sank down beside him, pulling an afghan that I'd brought from the house over both of us. He grasped my hand the way the children used to when I'd comfort them after bad nightmares.

A nightmare, that's what today was.

"Melissa," he said after a moment, "why did you think I poisoned you?"

"It isn't important now." We'd have to talk about it, of course, but later, when we were both stronger. I'd have to finally confront him about Jake. After that . . .

"No, please, I need to know."

". . . After Jake . . . died . . ."

"Jake? What does his death have to do with this?"

"I was there, Ray. I saw the two of you struggling in mid air."

His lips twisted and he let go of my hand. "The son of a bitch tried to kill me."

"Jake, kill *you?* He was your friend; you meant a lot to him."

"He was your lover."

142

"No, *my* friend too. All we ever did when we were alone together was talk about you and why our marriage was dying."

A spasm overcame him, and he made a choking sound. When he recovered he didn't speak. I felt a coldness in him — anger, too, directed at me. And suddenly I understood.

"Oh, no!" I said. "You think Jake tried to kill you because of me. You think we conspired to get rid of you!"

His pain-dull eyes watched me for a moment. "You didn't plan to kill me? And you weren't sleeping with him?"

"I told you I wasn't. I've slept with exactly two men other than you in my life — the last over five years ago. And even if I had been having an affair with Jake, I would never have plotted to hurt you." The tears I'd been controlling started again.

Ray put a shaky hand to my cheek, tried to brush them away. "What've I been thinking? Accusing you over and over. And today . . . I thought you'd decided you couldn't go on without Jake and were going to — Christ, what a hideous, twisted imagination I've got!"

"No more than mine. I thought *you* killed Jake and were faking your illness so I wouldn't realize you'd poisoned me."

He shook his head, grimacing. "You know, this would be funny if it wasn't so . . ."

"Yes."

We sat silently for a while. A distant thrumming and flapping noise came from beyond the pine-covered hills to the west.

"What about Jake?" Ray asked. "Why did he grab at my chute like that? There has to be a reason." He closed his eyes, probably reliving the horrifying experience. "Oh, God," he said heavily.

"What?"

143

"Jake taught skydiving, remember. Instructors are trained to notice things that other divers might not. He wasn't trying to kill me — he was trying to save my life. He must've seen something that told him my chute wasn't going to open. And he saved me at the expense of himself."

Ray lowered his face into his hands and made a strange sound. At first I couldn't identify it; then I realized he was crying. I'd never seen him shed so much as a single tear.

I peeled his hands away, took his face in both of mine, and kissed him. No words could ease the grief and shame we were feeling. There were not enough words to do that.

RAY

We were both composed again by the time the med-evac helicopter arrived. Huddled together under the afghan, holding hands. We hadn't said much after the revelations about Jake Hollis's death; there was only one issue left to discuss, and neither of us was quite ready to put it into words.

Every time I looked at her now, it was as if twenty-six years had melted away. I felt the same deep stirrings as that first night at her sorority's open house. But it wasn't a young woman's vulnerable beauty that attracted me this time, made me feel alive again; it was a mature woman's strength, compassion, capacity for giving and understanding. For such a long time I'd seen only the young Melissa whenever I looked at my wife — an illusion that had begun as reality and gradually evolved into pure fantasy. False illusion was what had driven the wedge between us, led to all the problems and foolish misconceptions we'd both had. And not only on my part; on hers too.

Neither of us knew each other any more. I wanted to know her again, everything there was to know about this Melissa — but did she feel the same about me? Did she

144

want to know the Ray Porter I'd grown and changed into, with all his flaws and insecurities? I thought I saw the answer in her eyes, but the spasms that continued to wrack us both made me unsure.

The helicopter was down finally, its rotors making a hell of a racket on the road out front. The paramedics would be here any minute. I had to get it out into the open now, before there was any more separation.

I squeezed her hand. "Melissa, it's not too late for us, is it? We can start over again, learn to love each other again?"

"I never stopped loving you," she said.

"Nor I you, but I mean —"

"I know what you mean. No more misunderstandings or misconceptions between us. No more walls."

"Yes."

"No more dying," she said, and now I was sure of what was in her eyes. "The dying time is over. Now we can start living again."

Part III:

Stories by
Bill Pronzini

Out of the Depths

He came tumbling out of the sea, dark and misshapen, like a being that was not human. A creature from the depths; or a jumbee, the evil spirit of West Indian superstition. Fanciful thoughts, and Shea was not a fanciful woman. But on this strange, wild night nothing seemed real or explicable.

At first, with the moon hidden behind the running scud of clouds, she'd seen him as a blob of flotsam on a breaking wave. The squall earlier had left the sea rough and the swells out toward the reef were high, their crests stripped of spume by the wind. The angry surf threw him onto the strip of beach, dragged him back again; another wave flung him up a little farther. The moon reappeared then, bathing sea and beach and rocks in the kind of frost-white shine you found only in the Caribbean. Not flotsam — something alive. She saw his arms extend, splayed fingers dig into the sand to hold himself against the backward pull of the sea. Saw him raise a smallish head above a massive, deformed torso, then squirm weakly toward the nearest jut of rock. Another wave shoved him the last few feet. He clung to the rock, lying motionless with the surf foaming around him.

Out of the depths, she thought.

The irony made her shiver, draw the collar of her coat more tightly around her neck. She lifted her gaze again to the rocky peninsula farther south. Windflaw Point, where the undertow off its tiny beach was the most treacherous on the island. It had taken her almost an hour to marshal her

149

courage to the point where she was ready — almost ready — to walk out there and into the ocean. *Into* the depths. Now . . .

Massive clouds sealed off the moon again. In the heavy darkness Shea could just make him out, still lying motionless on the fine coral sand. Unconscious? Dead? I ought to go down there, she thought. But she could not seem to lift herself out of the chair.

After several minutes he moved again: dark shape rising to hands and knees, then trying to stand. Three tries before he was able to keep his legs from collapsing under him. He stood swaying, as if gathering strength; finally staggered onto the path that led up through rocks and sea grape. Toward the house. Toward her.

On another night she would have felt any number of emotions by this time: surprise, bewilderment, curiosity, concern. But not on this night. There was a numbness in her mind, like the numbness in her body from the cold wind. It was as if she were dreaming, sitting there on the open terrace — as if she'd fallen asleep hours ago, before the clouds began to pile up at sunset and the sky turned the color of a blood bruise.

A new storm was making up. Hammering northern this time, from the look of the sky. The wind had shifted, coming out of the northeast now; the clouds were bloated and simmering in that direction and the air had a charged quality. Unless the wind shifted again soon, the rest of the night would be even wilder.

Briefly the clouds released the moon. In its white glare she saw him plodding closer, limping, almost dragging his left leg. A man, of course — just a man. And not deformed: what had made him seem that way was the life jacket fastened around his upper body. She remembered the lights of a freighter or tanker she had seen passing on the horizon just after nightfall, ahead of the squall. Had he gone overboard from that somehow?

He had reached the garden, was making his way past the flamboyant trees and the thick clusters of frangipani. Heading toward the garden door and the kitchen: she'd left the lights on in there and the jalousies open. It was the lights that had drawn him here, like a beacon that could be seen a long distance out to sea.

A good thing she'd left them on or not? She didn't want him here, a cast-up stranger, hurt and needing attention — not on this night, not when she'd been so close to making the walk to Windflaw Point. But neither could she refuse him access or help. John would have, if he'd been drunk and in the wrong mood. Not her. It was not in her nature to be cruel to anyone, except perhaps herself.

Abruptly Shea pushed herself out of the chair. He hadn't seen her sitting in the restless shadows, and he didn't see her now as she moved back across the terrace to the sliding glass doors to her bedroom. Or at least if he did see her, he didn't stop or call out to her. She hurried through the darkened bedroom, down the hall, and into the kitchen. She was halfway to the garden door when he began pounding on it.

She unlocked and opened the door without hesitation. He was propped against the stucco wall, arms hanging and body slumped with exhaustion. Big and youngish, that was her first impression. She couldn't see his face clearly.

"Need some help," he said in a thick, strained voice. "Been in the water . . . washed up on your beach. . . ."

"I know, I saw you from the terrace. Come inside."

"Better get a towel first. Coral ripped a gash in my foot . . . blood all over your floor."

"All right. I'll have to close the door. The wind. . . ."

"Go ahead."

She shut the door and went to fetch a towel, a blanket, and the first-aid kit. On the way back to the kitchen she turned the heat up several degrees. When she opened up to him again she saw that he'd shed the life jacket. His clothing was minimal: plaid wool shirt, denim trousers, canvas shoes, all nicked and torn by coral. Around his waist was a pouch-type waterproof belt, like a workman's utility belt. One of the pouches bulged slightly.

She gave him the towel, and when he had it wrapped around his left foot he hobbled inside. She took his arm, let him lean on her as she guided him to the kitchen table. His flesh was cold, sea-puckered; the touch of it made her feel a tremor of revulsion. It was like touching the skin of a dead man.

When he sank heavily onto one of the chairs, she dragged another chair over and lifted his injured leg onto it. He stripped off what was left of his shirt, swaddled himself in the blanket. His teeth were chattering.

The coffeemaker drew her; she poured two of the big mugs full. There was always hot coffee ready and waiting, no matter what the hour — she made sure of that. She drank too much coffee, much too much, but it was better than drinking what John usually drank. If she —

"You mind sweetening that?"

She half-turned. "Sugar?"

"Liquor. Rum, if you have it?"

"Jamaican rum." That was what John drank.

"Best there is. Fine."

She took down an open bottle, carried it and the mugs to the table, and watched while he spiked the coffee, drank, then poured more rum and drank again. Color came back into his stubbled cheeks. He used part of the blanket to rough-dry his hair.

He was a little older than she, early thirties, and in good physical condition: broad chest and shoulders, muscle-knotted arms. Sandy hair cropped short, thick sandy brows, a long-chinned face burned dark from exposure to the sun. The face was all right, might have been attractive except for the eyes. They were a bright off-blue color, shielded by lids that seemed perpetually lowered like flags at half-mast, and they didn't blink much. When the eyes lifted to meet and hold hers something in them made her look away.

"I'll see what I can do for your foot."

"Thanks. Hurts like hell."

The towel was already soaking through. Shea unwrapped it carefully, revealing a deep gash across the instep just above the tongue of his shoe. She got the shoe and sock off. More blood welled out of the cut.

"It doesn't look good. You may need a doctor —"

"No," he said, "no doctor."

"It'll take stitches to close properly."

"Just clean and bandage it, okay?"

She spilled iodine onto a gauze pad, swabbed at the gash as gently as she could. The sharp sting made him suck in his breath, but he didn't flinch or utter another sound. She laid a second piece of iodined gauze over the wound and began to wind tape tightly around his foot to hold the skin flaps together.

He said, "My name's Tanner. Harry Tanner."

"Shea Clifford."

"Shea. That short for something?"

"It's a family name."

"Pretty."

"Thank you."

"So are you," he said. "Real pretty with your hair all windblown like that."

She glanced up at him. He was smiling at her. Not a leer, just a weary smile, but it wasn't a good kind of smile. It had a predatory look, like the teeth-baring stretch of a wolf's jowls

"No offense," he said.

"None taken." She lowered her gaze, watched her hands wind and tear tape. Her mind still felt numb. "What happened to you? Why were you in the water?"

"That damn squall a few hours ago. Came up so fast I didn't have time to get my genoa down. Wave as big as a house knocked poor little *Wanderer* into a full broach. I got thrown clear when she went over or I'd have sunk with her."

"Were you sailing alone?"

"All alone."

"Single-hander? Or just on a weekend lark?"

"Single-hander. You know boats, I see."

"Yes. Fairly well."

"Well, I'm a sea tramp," Tanner said. "Ten years of island-hopping and this is the first time I ever got caught unprepared."

"It happens. What kind of craft was *Wanderer*?"

"Bugeye ketch. Thirty-nine feet."

"Shame to lose a boat like that."

He shrugged. "She was insured."

"How far out were you?"

"Five or six miles. Hell of a long swim in a choppy sea."

"You're lucky the squall passed as quickly as it did."

"Lucky I was wearing my life jacket, too," Tanner said. "And lucky you stay up late with your lights on. If it weren't for the lights I probably wouldn't have made shore at all."

Shea nodded. She tore off the last piece of tape and then

began putting the first-aid supplies away in the kit.

Tanner said, "I didn't see any other lights. This house the only one out here?"

"The only one on this side of the bay, yes."

"No close neighbors?"

"Three houses on the east shore, not far away."

"You live here alone?"

"With my husband."

"But he's not here now."

"Not now. He'll be home soon."

"That so? Where is he?"

"In Merrywing, the town on the far side of the island. He went out to dinner with friends."

"While you stayed home."

"I wasn't feeling well earlier."

"Merrywing. Salt Cay?"

"That's right."

"British-owned, isn't it?"

"Yes. You've never been here before?"

"Not my kind of place. Too small, too quiet, too rich. I prefer the livelier islands — St. Thomas, Nassau, Jamaica."

"St. Thomas isn't far from here," Shea said. "Is that where you were heading?"

"More or less. This husband of yours — how big is he?"

". . . Big?"

"Big enough so his clothes would fit me?"

"Oh," she said, "yes. About your size."

"Think he'd mind if you let me have a pair of his pants and a shirt and some underwear? Wet things of mine are giving me a chill."

"No, of course not. I'll get them from his room."

She went to John's bedroom. The smells of his cologne and pipe tobacco were strong in there; they made her faintly nauseous. In haste she dragged a pair of white linen trousers and a pullover off hangers in his closet, turned toward the dresser as she came out. And stopped in midstride.

Tanner stood in the open doorway, leaning against the jamb, his half-lidded eyes fixed on her.

"*His* room," he said. "Right."

"Why did you follow me?"

"Felt like it. So you don't sleep with him."

"Why should that concern you?"

"I'm naturally curious. How come? I mean, how come you and your husband don't share a bed?"

"Our sleeping arrangements are none of your business."

"Probably not. Your idea or his?"

"What?"

"Separate bedrooms. Your idea or his?"

"Mine, if you must know."

"Maybe he snores, huh?"

She didn't say anything.

"How long since you kicked him out of your bed?"

"I didn't kick him out. It wasn't like that."

"Sure it was. I can see it in your face."

"My private affairs —"

"— are none of my business. I know. But I also know the signs of a bad marriage when I see them. A bad marriage and an unhappy woman. Can't tell me you're not unhappy."

"All right," she said.

"So why don't you divorce him? Money?"

"Money has nothing to do with it."

"Money has something to do with everything."

"It isn't money."

"He have something on you?"

"No."

"Then why not just dump him?"

156

You're not going to divorce me, Shea. Not you, not like the others. I'll see you dead first. I mean it, Shea. You're mine and you'll stay mine until I decide I don't want you anymore. . . .

She said flatly, "I'm not going to talk about my marriage to you. I don't know you."

"We can fix that. I'm an easy guy to know."

She moved ahead to the dresser, found underwear and socks, put them on the bed with the trousers and pullover. "You can change in here," she said, and started for the doorway.

Tanner didn't move.

"I said —"

"I heard you, Shea."

"Mrs. Clifford."

"Clifford," he said. Then he smiled, the same wolfish lip-stretch he'd shown her in the kitchen. "Sure — Clifford. Your husband's name wouldn't be John, would it? John Clifford?"

She was silent.

"I'll bet it is. John Clifford, Clifford Yacht Designs. One of the best marine architects in Miami. Fancy motor sailers and racing yawls."

She still said nothing.

"House in Miami Beach, another on Salt Cay — this house. And you're his latest wife. Which is it, number three or number four?"

Between her teeth she said, "Three."

"He must be what, fifty now? And worth millions. Don't tell me money's not why you married him."

"I won't tell you anything."

But his wealth wasn't why she'd married him. He had been kind and attentive to her at first. And she'd been lonely after the bitter breakup with Neal. John had opened

157

up a whole new, exciting world to her: travel to exotic places, sailing, the company of interesting and famous people. She hadn't loved him, but she had been fond of him; and she'd convinced herself she would learn to love him in time. Instead, when he revealed his dark side to her, she had learned to hate him.

Tanner said, "Didn't one of his other wives divorce him for knocking her around when he was drunk? Seems I remember reading something like that in the Miami papers a few years back. That why you're unhappy, Shea? He knock *you* around when he's drinking?"

Without answering, Shea pushed past him into the hallway. He didn't try to stop her. In the kitchen again she poured yet another cup of coffee and sat down with it. Even with her coat on and the furnace turned up, she was still cold. The heat from the mug failed to warm her hands.

She knew she ought to be afraid of Harry Tanner. But all she felt inside was deep weariness. An image of Windflaw Point, the tiny beach with its treacherous undertow, flashed across the screen of her mind — and was gone again just as swiftly. Her courage, or maybe her cowardice, was gone too. She was no longer capable of walking out to the point, letting the sea have her. Not tonight and probably not ever again.

She sat listening to the wind clamor outside. It moaned in the twisted branches of the banyan tree; scraped palm fronds against the roof tiles. Through the open window jalousies she could smell ozone mixed with the sweet fragrances of white ginger blooms. The new storm would be here soon in all its fury.

The wind kept her from hearing Tanner reenter the kitchen. She sensed his presence, looked up, and saw him standing there with his eyes on her like probes. He'd put on

158

all of John's clothing and found a pair of Reeboks for his feet. In his left hand he held the waterproof belt that had been strapped around his waist.

"Shirt's a little snug," he said, "but a pretty good fit otherwise. Your husband's got nice taste."

Shea didn't answer.

"In clothing, in houses, and in women."

She sipped her coffee, not looking at him.

Tanner limped around the table and sat down across from her. When he laid the belt next to the bottle of rum, the pouch that bulged made a thunking sound. "Boats too," he said. "I'll bet he keeps his best designs for himself; he's the kind that would. Am I right, Shea?"

"Yes."

"How many boats does he own?"

"Two."

"One's bound to be big. Oceangoing yacht?"

"Seventy-foot custom schooner."

"What's her name?"

"*Moneybags*."

Tanner laughed. "Some sense of humor."

"If you say so."

"Where does he keep her? Here or Miami?"

"Miami."

"She there now?"

"Yes."

"And the other boat? That one berthed here?"

"The harbor at Merrywing."

"What kind is she?"

"A sloop," Shea said. "*Carib Princess*."

"How big?"

"Thirty-two feet."

"She been back and forth across the Stream?"

159

"Several times, in good weather."

"With you at the helm?"

"No."

"You ever take her out by yourself?"

"No. He wouldn't allow it."

"But you can handle her, right? You said you know boats. You can pilot that little sloop without any trouble?"

"Why do you want to know that? Why are you asking so many questions about John's boats?"

"John's boats, John's houses, John's third wife." Tanner laughed again, just a bark this time. The wolfish smile pulled his mouth out of shape. "Are you afraid of me, Shea?"

"No."

"Not even a little?"

"Why? Should I be?"

"What do you think?"

"I'm not afraid of you," she said.

"Then how come you lied to me?"

"Lied? About what?"

"Your husband. Old John Clifford."

"I don't know what you mean."

"You said he'd be home soon. But he won't be. He's not in town with friends, he's not even on the island."

She stared silently at the steam rising from her cup. Her fingers felt cramped, as if she might be losing circulation in them.

"Well, Shea? That's the truth, isn't it."

"Yes. That's the truth."

"Where is he? Miami?"

She nodded.

"Went there on business and left you all by your lonesome."

160

"It isn't the first time."

"Might be the last, though." Tanner reached for the rum bottle, poured some of the dark liquid into his mug, drank, and then smacked his lips. "You want a shot of this?"

"No."

"Loosen you up a little."

"I don't need loosening up."

"You might after I tell you the truth about Harry Tanner."

"Does that mean you lied to me too?"

"I'm afraid so. But you 'fessed up and now it's my turn."

In the blackness outside the wind gusted sharply, banging a loose shutter somewhere at the front of the house. Rain began to pelt down with open-faucet suddenness.

"Listen to that," Tanner said. "Sounds like we're in for a big blow, this time."

"What did you lie about?"

"Well, let's see. For starters, about how I came to be in the water tonight. My bugeye ketch didn't sink in the squall. No, *Wanderer*'s tied up at a dock in Charlotte Amalie."

She sat stiffly, waiting.

"Boat I was on didn't sink either," Tanner said. "At least as far as I know it didn't. I jumped overboard. Not long after the squall hit us."

There was still nothing for her to say.

"If I hadn't gone overboard, the two guys I was with would've shot me dead. They tried to shoot me in the water but the ketch was pitching like crazy and they couldn't see me in the dark and the rain. I guess they figured I'd drown even with a life jacket on. Or the sharks or barracuda would get me."

Still nothing.

"We had a disagreement over money. That's what most

161

things come down to these days — money. They thought I cheated them out of twenty thousand dollars down in Jamaica, and they were right, I did. They both put guns on me before I could do anything and I thought I was a dead man. The squall saved my bacon. Big swell almost broached us, knocked us all off our feet. I managed to scramble up the companionway and go over the side before they recovered."

The hard beat of the rain stopped as suddenly as it had begun. Momentary lull: the full brunt of the storm was minutes away yet.

"I'm not a single-hander," he said, "not a sea tramp. That's another thing I lied about. Ask me what it is I really am, Shea. Ask me how I make my living."

"I don't have to ask."

"No? Think you know?"

"Smuggling. You're a smuggler."

"That's right. Smart lady."

"Drugs, I suppose."

"Drugs, weapons, liquor, the wretched poor yearning to breathe free without benefit of a green card. You name it, I've handled it. Hell, smuggling's a tradition in these waters. Men have been doing it for three hundred years, since the days of the Spanish Main." He laughed. "A modern freebooter, that's what I am. Tanner the Pirate. Yo ho ho and a bottle of rum."

"Why are you telling me all this?"

"Why not? Don't you find it interesting?"

"No."

"Okay, I'll give it to you straight. I've got a problem — a big problem. I jumped off that ketch tonight with one thing besides the clothes on my back, and it wasn't money." He pulled the waterproof belt to him, unsnapped the pouch that bulged, and showed her what was inside. "Just this."

Her gaze registered the weapon — automatic, large caliber, lightweight frame — and slid away. She was not surprised; she had known there was a gun in the pouch when it made the thunking sound.

Tanner set it on the table within easy reach. "My two partners got my share of a hundred thousand from the Jamaica run. I might be able to get it back from them and I might not; they're a couple of hard cases and I'm not sure it's worth the risk. But I can't do anything until I quit this island. And I can't leave the usual ways because my money and my passport are both on that damn ketch. You see my dilemma, Shea?"

"I see it."

"Sure you do. You're a smart lady, like I said. What else do you see? The solution?"

She shook her head.

"Well, I've got a dandy." The predatory grin again. "You know, this really is turning into my lucky night. I couldn't have washed up in a better spot if I'd planned it. John Clifford's house, John Clifford's smart and pretty wife. And not far away, John Clifford's little sloop, the *Carib Princess*."

The rain came again, wind-driven with enough force to rattle the windows. Spray blew in through the screens behind the open jalousies. Shea made no move to get up and close the glass. Tanner didn't even seem to notice the moisture.

"Here's what we're going to do," he said. "At dawn we'll drive in to the harbor. You do have a car here? Sure you do; he wouldn't leave you isolated without wheels. Once we get there we go on-board the sloop and you take her out. If anybody you know sees us and says anything, you tell them I'm a friend or relative and John said it was okay

163

for us to go for a sail without him."

She asked dully, "Then what?"

"Once we're out to sea? I'm not going to kill you and dump your body overboard, if that's worrying you. The only thing that's going to happen is we sail the *Carib Princess* across the Stream to Florida. A little place I know on the west coast up near Pavilion Key where you can sneak a boat in at night and keep her hidden for as long as you need to."

"And then?"

"Then I call your husband and we do some business. How much do you think he'll pay to get his wife and his sloop back safe and sound? Five hundred thousand? As much as a million?"

"My God," she said. "You're crazy."

"Like a fox."

"You couldn't get away with it. You *can't*."

"I figure I can. You think he won't pay because the marriage is on the rocks? You're wrong, Shea. He'll pay, all right. He's the kind that can't stand losing anything that belongs to him, wife or boat, and sure as hell not both at once. Plus he's had enough bad publicity; ignoring a ransom demand would hurt his image and his business and I'll make damned sure he knows it."

She shook her head again a limp, rag-doll wobbling, as if it were coming loose from the stem of her neck.

"Don't look so miserable," Tanner said cheerfully. "I'm not such a bad guy when you get to know me, and there'll be plenty of time for us to get acquainted. And when old John pays off, I'll leave you with the sloop and you can sail her back to Miami. Okay? Give you my word on that."

He was lying: his word was worthless. He'd told her his name, the name of his ketch and where it was berthed; he

164

wouldn't leave her alive to identify him. Not on the Florida coast. Not even here.

Automatically Shea picked up her mug, tilted it to her mouth. Dregs. Empty. She pushed back her chair, crossed to the counter, and poured the mug full again. Tanner sat relaxed, smiling, pleased with himself. The rising steam from the coffee formed a screen between them, so that she saw him as blurred, distorted. Not quite human, the way he had first seemed to her when he came out of the sea earlier.

Jumbee, she thought. Smiling evil.

The gale outside flung sheets of water at the house. The loose shutter chattered like a jackhammer until the wind slackened again.

Tanner said, "Going to be a long wet night." He made a noisy yawning sound. "Where do you sleep, Shea?"

The question sent a spasm through her body.

"Your bedroom — where is it?"

Oh God. "Why?"

"I told you, it's going to be a long night. And I'm tired and my foot hurts and I want to lie down. But I don't want to lie down alone. We might as well start getting to know each other the best way there is."

No, she thought. No, no, no.

"Well, Shea? Lead the way."

No, she thought again. But her legs worked as if with a will of their own, carried her back to the table. Tanner sat forward as she drew abreast of him, started to lift himself out of the chair.

She pivoted and threw the mug of hot coffee into his face.

She hadn't planned to do it, acted without thinking; it was almost as much of a surprise to her as it was to him. He yelled and pawed at his eyes, his body jerking so violently

165

that both he and the chair toppled over sideways. Shea swept the automatic off the table and backed away with it extended at arm's length.

Tanner kicked the chair away and scrambled unsteadily to his feet. Bright red splotches stained his cheeks where the coffee had scalded him; his eyes were murderous. He took a step toward her, stopped when he realized she was pointing his own weapon at him. She watched him struggle to regain control of himself and the situation.

"You shouldn't have done that, Shea."

"Stay where you are."

"That gun isn't loaded."

"It's loaded. I know guns too."

"You won't shoot me." He took another step.

"I will. Don't come any closer."

"No you won't. You're not the type. I can pull the trigger on a person real easy. Have, more than once." Another step. "But not you. You don't have what it takes."

"Please don't make me shoot you. Please, please don't."

"See? You won't do it because you can't."

"Please."

"You won't shoot me, Shea."

On another night, any other night, he would have been right. But on this night —

He lunged at her.

And she shot him.

The impact of the high-caliber bullet brought him up short, as if he had walked into an invisible wall. A look of astonishment spread over his face. He took one last convulsive step before his hands came up to clutch at his chest and his knees buckled.

Shea didn't see him fall; she turned away. And the hue and the cry of the storm kept her from hearing him hit the

166

floor. When she looked again, after several seconds, he lay face down and unmoving on the tiles. She did not have to go any closer to tell that he was dead.

There was a hollow queasiness in her stomach. Otherwise she felt nothing. She turned again, and there was a blank space of time, and then she found herself sitting on one of the chairs in the living room. She would have wept then but she had no tears. She had cried herself dry on the terrace.

After a while she became aware that she still gripped Tanner's automatic. She set it down on an end table; hesitated, then picked it up again. The numbness was finally leaving her mind, a swift release that brought her thoughts into sharpening focus. When the wind and rain lulled again she stood, walked slowly down the hall to her bedroom. She steeled herself as she opened the door and turned on the lights.

From where he lay sprawled across the bed, John's sightless eyes stared up at her. The stain of blood on his bare chest, drying now, gleamed darkly in the lamp glow.

Wild night, mad night.

She hadn't been through hell just once, she'd been through it twice. First in here and then in the kitchen.

But she hadn't shot John. She hadn't. He'd come home at nine, already drunk, and tried to make love to her, and when she denied him he'd slapped her, kept slapping her. After three long hellish years she couldn't take it anymore, not anymore. She'd managed to get the revolver out of her nightstand drawer . . . not to shoot him, just as a threat to make him leave her alone. But he'd lunged at her, in almost the same way Tanner had, and they'd struggled, and the gun had gone off. And John Clifford was dead.

She had started to call the police. Hadn't because she

167

knew they would not believe it was an accident. John was well liked and highly respected on Salt Cay; his public image was untarnished and no one, not even his close friends, believed his second wife's divorce claim or that he could ever mistreat anyone. She had never really been accepted here — some of the cattier rich women thought she was a gold digger — and she had no friends of her own in whom she could confide. John had seen to that. There were no marks on her body to prove it, either; he'd always been very careful not to leave marks.

The island police would surely have claimed she'd killed him in cold blood. She'd have been arrested and tried and convicted and put in a prison much worse than the one in which she had lived the past three years. The prospect of that was unbearable. It was what had driven her out onto the terrace, to sit and think about the undertow at Windflaw Point. The sea, in those moments, had seemed her only way out.

Now there was another way.

Her revolver lay on the floor where it had fallen. John had given it to her when they were first married, because he was away so much; and he had taught her how to use it. It was one of three handguns he'd bought illegally in Miami.

Shea bent to pick it up. With a corner of the bedsheet she wiped the grip carefully, then did the same to Tanner's automatic. That gun too, she was certain, would not be registered anywhere.

Wearily she put the automatic in John's hand, closing his fingers around it. Then she retreated to the kitchen and knelt to place the revolver in Tanner's hand. The first-aid kit was still on the table; she would use it once more, when she finished talking to the chief constable in Merrywing.

We tried to help Tanner, John and I, she would tell him.

And he repaid our kindness by attempting to rob us at gunpoint. John told him we kept money in our bedroom; he took the gun out of the nightstand before I could stop him. They shot each other. John died instantly, but Tanner didn't believe his wound was as serious as it was. He made me bandage it and then kept me in the kitchen, threatening to kill me too. I managed to catch him off guard and throw coffee in his face. When he tried to come after me the strain aggravated his wound and he collapsed and died.

If this were Miami, or one of the larger Caribbean islands, she could not hope to get away with such a story. But here the native constabulary was unsophisticated and inexperienced because there was so little crime on Salt Cay. They were much more likely to overlook the fact that John had been shot two and a half hours before Harry Tanner. Much more likely, too, to credit a double homicide involving a stranger, particularly when they investigated Tanner's background, than the accidental shooting of a respected resident who had been abusing his wife. Yes, she might just get away with it. If there was any justice left for her in this world, she would — and one day she'd leave Salt Cay a free woman again.

Out of the depths, she thought as she picked up the phone. Out of the depths. . . .

Man on the Run

When Harry Dice finally caught up with me I was in Washington state, working the cranberry bogs on the Long Beach peninsula.

It was mid-October and I'd been there nearly three months, at least a month longer than it was safe to stay in any one place. A big mistake to hang on that long, but there were reasons why I'd done it. I was tired of running, that was one. Another: I hated having to leave Anne, the first woman I'd cared anything about since Fay. Another: I didn't want to let Ev Cotter down; the cranberry harvest was due in a week, and the growers needed all the help they could get. Another: Long Beach was the first place I'd been in twenty-nine years of rambling and scrambling that felt like a home to me.

Cold, the morning Dice showed up. Blustery wind off the Pacific, whipping across the peninsula to rumple the surface of Shoalwater Bay. The land finger is fourteen miles long, but only about two miles wide for most of its length; if it weren't flattish and heavily wooded with pine and cedar, you could stand in the middle of it and see both the long stretches of beach on the ocean side and the Shoalwater and Willapa Bay shorelines on the inland side. The locals call it "Cape Cod of the West," because of its shape and the cranberries and a heavy summer population.

I was out in Cotter's bogs, on the slender levee road between #6 field and #7 field, finishing up the last of the mowing. The sunken bogs were all reddish stubble now, ready for next week's flooding and harvesting. The cranberry harvest is a big deal in Long Beach; 550 acres of cranberries are grown on the peninsula, almost ten percent of the entire West Coast production. I was looking forward to it. If you'd said to me three or four years ago that before I turned thirty I'd get a kick out of standing hip-deep in freezing water, scooping off floating berries with a long wooden paddle, I'd have laughed in your face. Rambling and scrambling changes people, I guess. Or maybe it's just that it takes some a hell of a lot longer than others to grow up.

I thought about Anne as I worked. She was a schoolteacher in Oysterville, the village on the northern tip; I'd met her in a supermarket two weeks after I hit Long Beach. And she was about as different from Fay as it was possible for two women to be. Anne was sweet, warm, gentle. Fay had been beautiful, hot, and hard — fire burning around a core of ice. Anne didn't smoke or drink; Fay had been a chain-smoker and an alcoholic. Anne did charity and volunteer work, cared about people, and wasn't much interested in the things money could buy. Fay hadn't given a damn about anybody but herself, took what she wanted when she wanted it, and loved the power of the almighty dollar as much as she loved Fay Dice.

With her it had been secret meetings and secret plans and body heat. With Anne it was movies, dinners, walks along the beach, sailboating on Willapa Bay — and a goodnight kiss when I took her home. I'd have laughed in your face once, too, if you'd told me a goodnight kiss and holding hands would be enough for me with any woman. It was best for Anne that things hadn't gotten too serious between us, but I regretted it just the same. And pretty soon now, despite how I felt, I'd have to leave her cold: no explanations, no goodbyes. It would hurt her, but what choice did I have? A man on the run —

"Hello, Maguire."

He said it loud, to make himself heard over the whine of the mower. I swung around and there he was, five feet away. Just standing there, all alone, watching me. Harry Dice.

A chill went up my back. In those first few seconds I had a crazy urge to cut and run, keep on running until he caught me or I dropped from exhaustion. But there was nowhere to go, not anymore. When the panic died I didn't feel much of anything. Funny. I'd had nightmares about coming face-to-face with him like this, and each time I'd woken up dripping with fear-sweat. Now that the moment had come, I wasn't afraid. The only feeling in me seemed to be a kind of distant relief that this part of it was finally over.

I shut off the mower. After that, neither of us moved for maybe a minute. Harry Dice. Bigshot criminal lawyer. Mob lawyer, with ties to one of the worst crime families in the Chicago area — but I hadn't known that until it was too late. I'd had contact with him less than a dozen times in Chicago, for about a minute each. We'd said less than a hundred words to each other; men like Dice don't have conversations with the attendants who park their cars. In my memory I'd built him up as a big man, imposing, powerful, a giant with eyes that could slice you up like knives — and he was none of those things. Just a middle-aged man in a camel's hair overcoat, hunch-shouldered, with saggy jowls and creases in his cheeks and eyes that were squinty and moist from the wind. Harry Dice in the flesh wasn't any less deadly; a little easier to face, was all, especially since he hadn't brought anybody with him.

"You don't seem surprised to see me," he said. His voice

was powerful enough — he was supposed to be hell-on-wheels in a courtroom — but there was a flatness, almost a dullness to the words. He had every reason to hate my guts, but there was no hate in his tone. Maybe that meant something. And maybe it didn't.

"No. The odds were all on your side, Mr. Dice."

"Three years is a long time to keep running."

"I figured it was better than the alternative."

"Easier on both of us if you hadn't managed to stay one jump ahead of the detectives I hired. They came close to grabbing you twice the first year."

"Detectives?" I said. "Is that what they are?"

"What did you think they were?"

I didn't say anything.

"You never stayed anywhere longer than two months," Dice said, "and yet you've been here almost three. I wonder why."

"I like it here."

"Is that the only reason?"

When I didn't answer he said, "Born in Chicago, weren't you?"

In a south-side slum. "You know where I was born, Mr. Dice."

"City boy," he said. "Urban environment most of your life until three years ago. I expected you to try losing yourself in a city, but the only one you've been to is Seattle for a couple of weeks."

"I guess I had enough of city living." And city people like Fay. And Harry Dice. And guys I grew up with who used crack and smack and died with bullets in their heads. And my mother, who never even knew my father's name.

"Cranberry bogs," he said, and shook his head. "There can't be much money in a job like this."

"Hardly any. But money isn't everything."

"You must have thought it was once, three years ago."

"Look, Mr. Dice —"

"Fifteen or sixteen jobs since you left Chicago, and every one menial. Took you two years to scrape together enough to buy that beat-up old Ford you drive."

"I never got any of that eighty-five thousand," I said. "Fay took it all when she left me. It burned up with her in the accident."

Noise had begun to fill the gray sky: honking and fluttering. It made Dice look up. Flock of Canada geese, flying in formation the way they always did, headed up over Shoalwater Bay for the wildlife refuge on Long Island. He watched them for a few seconds before he put his eyes on me again.

"I don't give a damn about the money," he said.

". . . You don't?"

"I never did."

"But I thought —"

"I don't care what you thought. Tell me, Maguire: Where were you when Fay died?"

My lips were dry from the wind; I licked them before I said, "On a bus halfway between Denver and Salt Lake City."

"So it was over between you and her by then?"

"All over. Finished."

"The car she was driving — you bought it in upstate Illinois in your name."

"I bought it, but she gave me the cash."

"And you let her take it in Denver. The car and the eighty-five thousand. Just like that."

"There wasn't any other choice."

His mouth opened, started to shape a word — the first

174

one of a question, maybe. Then he seemed to shake himself. When he spoke again I had the feeling it wasn't what he'd been about to say before.

"The two of you didn't even last a week together."

"No, not even a week."

"How long were you sleeping with her in Chicago?"

"Six weeks. Seven. I don't remember."

"It meant that little to you?"

"It meant plenty in the beginning."

"Did it? Were you in love with her?"

"I thought I was. I mean that, Mr. Dice."

"Was she in love with you?"

"Same thing. She thought she was, or tried to talk herself into believing she was."

"Whose idea for the two of you to run off together?"

"Hers."

"Whose idea to take the money out of my safe?"

"Hers. I didn't know it was so much until we got to Denver. She said she was only going to take a small amount — five thousand or so to get us started."

"Would you have gone if you'd known how much she did take? Or if there'd been no money at all?"

I said, "I don't know," and the words put a thin, humorless smile on Dice's mouth. He knew that was a lie. The "five thousand or so" was the reason I'd let her talk me into going. Just that much was more than I'd ever thought I would get close to in one lump. Eighty-five thousand was too much; it scared hell out of me then and still did now.

Dice said, "Tell me the whys, Maguire. I need to know."

"The whys?"

"Why did Fay want to get away from me so badly? Why did she pick a man like you, a parking-garage attendant? Why any of it?"

"I don't know why she picked me. I was there, I guess. Available and dumb enough to be willing."

"You weren't her first lover, you know. She had at least three others."

I hadn't known that. But it didn't surprise me; it would have if I'd been the only one.

"But she didn't run away with them," Dice said. "Just you."

"She said she was afraid to stay with you. That's the reason she wanted out."

The words seemed to sting him; he winced and hunched more tightly inside his coat. "Afraid of me? For God's sake, I never harmed or even threatened her. I loved her, Maguire — I mean I really loved her. You understand?"

"Yes, sir, I understand."

"I gave her everything she wanted. I treated her like a goddess. What did she have to be afraid of?"

"She let me think you abused her. She didn't tell me the truth until after we quit Chicago."

"Truth?"

"It wasn't you she was scared of — it was your clients, the people you work for."

"My God," Dice said.

"She thought you were in too deep. That's what she said. In too deep, and bound to make a mistake some day and then they'd hurt you. Or her to get back at you."

"She was wrong."

"Well, she didn't think so."

"My practice isn't like that. I've defended men involved in organized crime, yes, but I don't take orders from any of them. I'm still my own man. I'm not in jeopardy and neither was she."

"I'm only telling you what she told me, Mr. Dice."

176

"Why didn't she come to me? Tell *me* her fears?"

"I don't know. All I know is, she was afraid and that's what started her drinking so much, and all she could think to do was to get out before it was too late, start a new life somewhere else."

"With you and eighty-five thousand dollars from my safe."

"She figured she was entitled to the money," I said. "A settlement, she called it."

"Settlement," he said. Then he said, "What ended it between the two of you in Denver? What she told you about my law practice?"

"Yeah. That, and how much money she'd taken. For all I knew, you'd sent Mob enforcers after us. I didn't want any part of that. I still don't."

"So you were the one who wanted out."

"We both wanted out by then. I told her the smart thing was for her to take the money, all of it, and go back to Chicago. No matter how bad she thought things were with you, being on the run by herself would be worse."

"What made you think I'd take her back?"

"She said you loved her, that was one thing she never doubted. You would've taken her back, wouldn't you?"

He didn't answer that. He said, "But she wouldn't listen, is that it? Hard-nosed Fay."

"Not at first. We argued about it for two days straight, both of us drinking too much, before I finally convinced her I was right. We split up the next morning. She took the car and the money and I caught the bus for Salt Lake."

"When did you find out about the accident?"

"Few days later. In one of the Chicago papers I got at a newsstand in Salt Lake."

"She was heading east when it happened. That's what

the Nebraska state police told me."

"Yeah. She always drove too fast, even when it was pouring down rain. . . ."

"Rain didn't cause the accident," Dice said. "She was drunk. Three times the legal Nebraska limit."

That was something else that didn't surprise me. But I let it pass without saying anything. The wind gusted; it made a sound in the cranberry stubble like decks of cards being shuffled. There was a funny look on Dice's face, one I couldn't read, and when he spoke again it was in a low voice that I could barely hear above the wind.

"Where was she going, Maguire?"

"Where? To Chicago."

"*Was* she coming back to me?" That was the question he'd started to ask earlier; I knew it as soon as I heard it.

"Sure she was."

"What makes you so sure?"

"She told me she was and I believed her."

"Because you'd finally convinced her it was her only option. Because she was even more afraid not to."

"It was more than that," I said. "She still cared for you. She never stopped caring — I could see that all along."

"Did she say she still cared?"

"Yeah. One of the last things she said before we split up was, 'We made a big mistake, Jack. I hope Harry can forgive me. I still care for him, and if he still loves me after this, maybe the two of us can work something out. It's the only hope I've got left now."

He looked at me for a long time, while the wind fluttered around us and one of the other workers fired up a mower. Then his head came up and his shoulders lost their hunch; he seemed to stand taller, like somebody who'd had a heavy weight lifted off him.

I said, "I'm sorry about Fay, Mr. Dice. I'm not just saying that — I mean it. I'm sorry any of it ever happened."

"All right."

I took a breath before I asked, "So what happens now?"

"Nothing happens. You go back to work and I go back to Chicago."

"And later tonight I get a visitor or two? A bullet in the head, Mr. Dice? Or just a wheelchair for the rest of my life?"

"You sound like a character in a cheap melodrama."

"Well, what am I supposed to think? You spent three years and plenty of money to track me down. It wasn't so we could have a ten-minute conversation."

"Yes, it was," he said. "So I could ask you the questions you just answered."

"I don't . . . questions?"

"Why Fay left with you. Whether or not she was coming back home when she died. If she still had any love left for me. I had to know, Maguire. You asked me if I'd have taken her back. The answer is yes, in a second. I'd have forgiven her anything, even you, to have her back. I've spent the past three years learning to live without her, but I doubt I could go on many more years without something positive to hang on to." He saw the look on my face and added, "You don't understand, do you?"

"Maybe I do."

"No, because you've never loved a woman the way I loved Fay. But I really don't care if you understand or not. The fact is I don't give any more of a damn about you than I do about the money. I don't hate you, I don't blame you — I don't have any feelings at all toward you."

I didn't feel anything either right then, not even relief. Later . . . all that would come later.

His eyes weren't on me any longer. He was staring down into #6 field. "Ironic, isn't it," he said, and I think it was as much to himself as to me.

"What is?"

"That it should end here, in a place like this. Same kind of place we've been in for three long years, you and me."

"I don't know what you mean, Mr. Dice."

"I mean," he said, "we can both stop running now."

And he put his back to me and walked away without looking back.

I quit the fields at five and drove straight to the motel in Ocean Park where I rented a room. I washed up, changed clothes, then lay on the bed and looked at the phone without picking it up. Anne would be home by now and I wanted to talk to her, but I didn't know yet what I would say. It didn't seem right, somehow, to just pretend nothing had changed, that today was the same as yesterday.

I felt the relief now, but nothing much else. No good feelings — just a kind of flatness. Three years. Three years of running, hiding, working at lousy jobs and living in lonely rooms like this one, and all Harry Dice had wanted was to ask me a few questions. He wasn't a killer or a Mafia bigshot on a vendetta; he was a poor sad bastard pining away for a dead love. Well, I'd made it easier for him and for myself in the bargain. I'd told him exactly what he wanted to hear.

The truth, partly. And half-truths and outright lies.

Fay hadn't been going back to him when she was killed on that rain-slick highway. She was still running — away from me as well as from him — and wherever she'd been running to, it hadn't been Chicago. She hadn't had any love left for Harry Dice, if she'd ever loved him in the first place.

She'd hated him. That was the real reason she'd run off with me and his money. The last thing she'd said to me was, "I'll never let him find me, Jack, and you better not ever let him find you. I'd die before I'd go back to Chicago. I hate his damn insides."

I'd had to let her take the car; she threatened to call Dice if I didn't, tell him I'd forced her to go away with me, abused her until she agreed, and she'd run out on me because she was tired of being kicked around. He'd come after me with a vengeance then, she said, kill me himself — and I believed it. When she left, she thought she was taking all the money with her too. But she was wrong. The two minutes she'd spent in the bathroom before walking out had made her wrong. I'd been afraid she would take it into her head to call Dice anyway, blame everything on me, and I was damned if I would let her get away with leaving me holding an empty bag. I wasn't thinking straight. I hadn't started thinking straight until I got to Salt Lake City.

The eighty-five thousand hadn't burned up in the car smash; it had been with me on the bus, two hundred miles away. Almost the entire amount was in a bank in Seattle right now, earning interest, and had been even before I found out Fay was dead.

Three years, and all I'd spent of it was a few hundred dollars. I'd been afraid to spend more. Afraid Dice would hunt even harder if he thought I was living it up on his money. Afraid to send it back to him because what if I really needed it someday, to leave the country? Afraid all the time, afraid of everything.

But now I didn't have to be afraid. Dice really didn't care about the money; he'd had no reason to lie to me about that. It was all mine and I could do what I wanted with it. Spend it on Anne . . . except that Anne had no interest in money or what it could buy. And I couldn't think of anything I wanted to buy for myself either. Not a single thing.

That was the reason for the flat feeling. Admit it, Maguire. Dice didn't care about the money, Anne wouldn't care, and after three years you don't care either.

In my mind I could see Dice standing on the levee road, staring down into the cranberry field. And I could hear him saying: *Ironic, isn't it? . . . That it should end here, in a place like this. Same kind of place we've been in for three long years, you and me.* I hadn't known then what he meant, but I knew now. Bogs. The two of us like men running in a swamp, weighted down with baggage and going nowhere, and if we'd kept up the chase much longer we'd have been mired so deep we'd never have gotten out.

The money and the fear were my baggage, just like Dice's love for Fay had been his. I'd gotten rid of the fear — and I could get rid of the money too. Anne's charity work: Eighty-five thousand plus interest would do a lot of needy people a lot of good. I could tell her I'd inherited it . . . no. No. Tell her the truth, the whole story. No more lies, especially not to Anne. No more baggage.

I sat up and reached for the phone. The flatness was gone; now I had the good feeling I'd been waiting for all day. I didn't have to leave Anne or Long Beach. Dice had been right: We could both stop running.

Home is the Place Where

A "Nameless Detective" Story

It was one of those little crossroads places you still find occasionally in the California backcountry. Relics of another era; old dying things, with precious little time left before they crumble into dust. Weathered wooden store building, gas pumps, a detached service garage that also housed restrooms, some warped little tourist cabins clustered close behind; a couple of junk-car husks and a stand of dusty shade trees. This one was down in the central part of the state, southeast of San Juan Bautista, on the way to the Pinnacles National Monument. The name on the pocked metal sign on the store roof was *Benson's Oasis*. There were four cabins and the shade trees were cottonwoods.

No other cars sat on the apron in front when I pulled in at a few minutes past two. Nor were there any vehicles back by the cabins. The only spot to hide one was in the detached garage — and it was shut up tight. Maybe something in that, maybe not.

Heat hammered at me when I got out, thick and deep-summer dry. In the distance, haze blurred the shapes of the brown hills of the Diablo Range. It was flat here, and dust-blown, and quiet. The feeling you had was of isolation, emptiness, and displacement in time. For me, it was a pleasant feeling, not at all unsettling. I like the past; I like it a hell of a lot better than I like the present or the prospects for the future.

It was even hotter inside the store. No air-conditioning, just an old-fashioned ceiling fan that stirred the air in a way that made me think of a ladle stirring bouillon. Under the fan flies floated in random lethargic circles, as if they'd been drugged. The old man behind the counter at the rear had the same drugged, listless aspect. He was perched on a stool, studying a book of some kind that was open on the countertop. A bell had tinkled to announce my arrival but at first he didn't look up. He turned a page as I crossed the room; it made a dry rustling sound. The page was black, with what looked to be photographs and paper items affixed to it. A scrapbook.

When I reached him he shut the book. It had a brown simulated leather cover, the word *Memories* embossed on it in gilt. The gilt had flaked and faded and the ersatz leather was cracked: the book was almost as old as he was. Over seventy, I judged. Thin, stoop-shouldered, white hair as fine as rabbit fur. Heavily seamed face. Bent left arm that was also knobbed and crooked at the wrist, as if it had been badly broken once and hadn't healed well.

"What can I do for you?" he asked.

"You're the owner? Everett Benson?"

"I am."

"I'm looking for your son, Mr. Benson."

No reaction.

"Have you seen him, heard from him, in the past two days?"

Still nothing for several seconds. Then, "I have no son."

"Stephen," I said. "Stephen Arthur Benson."

"No."

"He's in trouble. Serious trouble."

Face like a chunk of eroded limestone, eyes like cloudy agates imbedded in it. "I have no son," he said again.

I took out one of my business cards, tried to give it to him. He wouldn't take it. Finally I laid it on the counter in front of him. "Stephen was in jail in San Francisco," I said, "on a charge of selling amphetamines and crack cocaine. Did you know that?"

Silence.

"He talked the woman he was living with into going to a bondsman and bailing him out. The bail was low and she had just enough collateral to swing it. His trial date was yesterday. Two nights ago he stole a hundred dollars from the woman, and her car, and jumped bail."

More silence.

"The bondsman hired me to find him and bring him back," I said. "I think he came here. You're his only living relative, and he needs more money than he's got to keep on running. He could steal it but it would be easier and safer to get it from you."

Benson pushed off his stool, picked up the scrapbook, laid it on a shelf behind him. Several regular hardback books lined the rest of the shelf, all of them old and well-read; in the weak light I couldn't make out any of the titles.

"Aiding and abetting a fugitive is a felony," I said to his back, "even if the fugitive is your own son. You don't want to get yourself in trouble with the law, do you?"

He said again, without turning, "I have no son."

For the moment I'd taken the argument as far as it would go. I left him and went out into the midday glare. And straight over to the closed-up service garage.

There were two windows along the near side, both dusty and speckled with ground-in dirt, but I could see clearly enough through the first. Sufficient daylight penetrated the gloom so I could identify the two vehicles parked in there. One was a dented, rusted, thirty-year-old Ford pickup that no doubt belonged to the old man. The other was a newish red Mitsubishi. I didn't have to see the license plate to know that the Mitsubishi belonged to Stephen Arthur Benson's girlfriend.

Cars drifted past on the highway; they made the only sound in the stillness. Behind the store, where the cabins were, nothing moved except for shimmers of heat. I went to my car, sleeving away sweat, and unclipped the short-barrelled .38 revolver from under the dash and slid it into the pocket of my suit jacket. Maybe I'd need the gun and maybe I wouldn't, but I felt better armed. Stephen Benson was a convicted felon and something of a hardcase, and for all I knew he was armed himself. He hadn't had a weapon two nights ago, according to the girlfriend, but he might have picked one up somewhere in the interim. From his father, for instance.

The stand of cottonwoods grew along the far side of the parking area. I moved over into them, made my way behind the two cabins on the south side. Both had blank rear walls and uncurtained side windows; I took my time approaching each. Their interiors were sparsely furnished, and empty of people and personal belongings.

The direct route to the other two cabins was across open ground. I didn't like the idea of that, so I went the long way — back through the trees, across in front of the store, around on the far side of the garage. It was an unnecessary precaution, as it turned out. The farthest of the northside cabins was also empty; the near one showed plenty of signs of occupancy — clothing, books, photographs, a hotplate, a small refrigerator — but there wasn't anybody in it. This was where the old man lived, I thought. The clothing was the type he would wear and the books were similar to the ones in the store.

Nothing to do now but to go back inside and brace him again. When I entered the store he was on his stool, eating a Milky Way in little nibbling bites. He had loose false teeth and on each bite they clicked like beads on a string.

"Where is he, Mr. Benson?"

No response. The cloudy agate eyes regarded me with the same lack of expression as before.

"I saw the car in the garage," I said. "It's the one Stephen stole from the woman in San Francisco, no mistake. Either he's still in this area or you gave him money and another car and he's on the road again. Which is it?"

He clicked and chewed; he didn't speak.

"All right then. You don't want to do this the easy way, we'll have to do it the hard way. I'll call the county police and have them come out here and look at the stolen car; then they'll charge you with aiding and abetting and with harboring stolen property. And your son will still get picked up and sent back to San Francisco to stand trial. It's only a matter of time."

Benson finished the candy bar; I couldn't tell if he was thinking over what I'd said, but I decided I'd give him a few more minutes in case he was. In the stillness, a refrigeration unit made a broken chattery hum. The heat-drugged flies droned and circled. A car drew up out front and a grumpy-looking citizen came in and bought two cans of soda pop and a bag of potato chips. "Hot as Hades out there," he said. Neither Benson nor I answered him.

When he was gone I said to the old man, "Last chance.

187

Where's Stephen?" He didn't respond, so I said, "I've got a car phone. I'll use that to call the sheriff," and turned and started out.

He let me get halfway to the door before he said, "You win, mister," in a dull, empty voice. "Not much point in keeping quiet about it. Like you said, it's only a matter of time."

I came back to the counter. "Now you're being smart. Where is he?"

"I'll take you to him."

"Just tell me where I can find him."

"No. I'll take you there."

Might be better at that, I thought, if Stephen's close by. Easier, less chance for trouble, with the old man along. I nodded, and Benson came out from behind the counter and crossed to where a sign hung in the window; he reversed the sign so that the word *Closed* faced outward. Then we went out and he locked up.

I asked him, "How far do we have to go?"

"Not far."

"I'll drive, you tell me where."

We got into the car. He directed me east on the county road that intersected the main highway. We rode in silence for about a mile. Benson sat stiff-backed, his hands gripping his knees, eyes straight ahead. In the hard daylight the knobbed bone on his left wrist looked as big as a plum.

Abruptly he said, " 'Home is the place where.' "

". . . How's that again?"

" 'Home is the place where, when you have to go there, they have to take you in.' "

I shrugged because the words didn't mean anything to me.

"Lines from a poem by Robert Frost," he said. " 'The Death of the Hired Man,' I think. You read Frost?"

"No."

"I like him. Makes sense to me, more than a lot of them."

I remembered the well-read books on the store shelf and in the cabin. A rural storekeeper who read poetry and admired Robert Frost. Well, why not? People don't fit into easy little stereotypes. In my profession, you learn not to lose sight of that fact.

Home is the place where, when you have to go there, they have to take you in. The words ran around inside my head like song lyrics. No, like a chant or an invocation — all subtle rhythm and gathering power. They made sense to me, too, on more than one level. Now I knew something more about Everett Benson, and something more about the nature of his relationship with his son.

Another couple of silent miles through sun-struck farmland. Alfalfa and wine grapes, mostly. A private farm road came up on the right; Benson told me to turn there. It had once been a good road, unpaved but well graded, but that had been a long time ago. Now there were deep grooves in it, and weeds and tall brown grass between the ruts. Not used much these days. It led along the shoulder of a sere hill, then up to the crest; from there I could see where it ended.

Benson's Oasis was a dying place, with not much time left. The farm down below was already dead — years dead. It had been built alongside a shallow creek where willows and cottonwoods grew, in the tuck where two hillocks came together: farmhouse, barn, two chicken coops, a shedlike outbuilding. Skeletons now, all of them, broken and half-hidden by high grass and shrubs and tangles of wild berry vines. Climbing primroses covered part of the house from foundation to roof, bright pink in the sunlight, like a gaudy fungus.

"Your property?" I asked him.

"Built it all with my own hands," he said. "After the war — Second World War — when land was cheap hereabouts. Raised chickens, alfalfa, apples. You can see there's still part of the orchard left."

There were a dozen or so apple trees, stretching away behind the barn. Gnarled, bent, twisted, but still producing fruit. Rotting fruit now.

"Moved out eight years ago, when my wife died," Benson said. "Couldn't bear to live here any more without Betty. Couldn't bear to sell the place, either." He paused, drew a heavy breath, let it out slowly. "Don't come out here much anymore. Just a couple of times a year to visit her grave."

There were no other cars in sight, but I could make out where one had angled off the roadway and mashed down an irregular swath of the summer-dead grass, not long ago. I followed the same route when we reached the farmyard. The swath stopped ten yards from what was left of the farmhouse's front porch. So did I.

I had my window rolled down but there was nothing to hear except birds and insects. The air was swollen with the smells of heat and dry grass and decaying apples.

I said, "Is he inside the house?"

"Around back."

"Where around back?"

"There's a beat-down path. Just follow that."

"You don't want to come along?"

"No need. I'll stay here."

I gave him a long look. There was no tension in him, no guile; not much emotion of any kind, it seemed. He just sat there, hands on knees, eyes front — the same posture he'd held throughout the short trip from the crossroads.

I thought about insisting he come with me, but something kept me from doing it. I got out, taking the keys from the ignition. Before I shut the door I drew the .38; then I leaned back in to look at Benson, holding the gun down low so he couldn't see it.

"You won't blow the horn or anything like that, will you?"

"No," he said, "I won't."

"Just wait quiet."

"Yes."

The beaten-down path was off to the right. I walked it slowly through the tangled vegetation, listening, watching my backtrail. Nothing made noise and nothing happened. The fermenting-apples smell grew stronger as I came around the house to the rear; bees swarmed back there, making a muted sawmill sound. Near where the orchard began, the path veered off toward the creek, toward a big weeping willow that grew on the bank.

And under the willow was where it ended: at the grave of Benson's wife, marked by a marble headstone etched with the words *Beloved Elizabeth — Rest in Eternal Peace.*

But hers was not the only grave there. Next to it was a second one, a new one, the earth so freshly turned some of the clods on top were still moist. That one bore no marker of any kind.

I went back to the car, not quite running. Benson was out of it now, standing a few feet away looking at the house and the climbing primroses. He turned when he heard me coming, faced me squarely as I neared him.

"Now you know," he said without emotion and without irony. "I didn't lie to you, mister. I have no son."

"Why didn't you tell me he was dead?"

"Wanted you to see it for yourself. His grave."

"How did he die?"

"I shot him," the old man said. "Last night, about ten o'clock."

"You shot him?"

"With my old Iver Johnson. Two rounds through the heart."

"Why? What happened?"

"He brought me trouble, just like before."

"You can state it plainer than that."

A little silence. Then, "He was bad, Stephen was. Mean and bad clear through. Always was, even as a boy. Stealing things, breaking up property, hurting other boys. Hurting his mother." Benson held up his crooked left arm. "Hurting me too."

"Stephen did that to you?"

"When he was eighteen. Broke my arm in three places. Two operations and it still wouldn't heal right."

"What made him do it?"

"I wouldn't give him the money he wanted. So he beat up on me to get it. I told him before he ran off, don't ever come back, you're not welcome in my house anymore. And he didn't come back, not in more than a dozen years. Not until last night, at the Oasis."

"He wanted money again, is that it? Tried to hurt you again when you wouldn't give it to him?"

"Punched me in the belly," Benson said. "Still hurts when I move sudden. So I went and got the Iver Johnson. He laughed when I pointed it at him and told him to get out. 'Won't shoot me, old man,' he said. 'Your own son. You won't shoot me.' "

"What did he do? Try to take the gun away from you?"

Benson nodded. "Didn't leave me any choice but to shoot him. Twice through the heart. Then I brought him out here and buried him next to his mother."

"Why did you do that?"

"I told you before. 'Home is the place where.' I had to take him in, didn't I? For the last time?"

The smell of the rotting apples seemed stronger now. And the heat was intense and the skeletal buildings and fungoid primroses were ugly. I didn't want to be here any longer — not another minute in this place.

"Get back in the car, Mr. Benson."

"Where we going?"

"Just get back in the car. Please."

He did what I told him. I backed the car around and drove up the hill and over it without glancing in the rear view mirror. Neither of us said anything until I swung off the county road, onto the apron in front of Benson's Oasis, and braked to a stop.

Then he asked, "You going to call the sheriff now?" Matter-of-factly; not as if he cared.

"No," I said.

"How come?"

"Stephen's dead and buried. I don't see any reason not to leave him right where he is."

"But I killed him. Shot him down like a dog."

Old and dying like his crossroads store, with precious little time left. Where was the sense — or the justice — in forcing him to die somewhere else? But all I said was, "You did what you had to do. I'll be going now. I've got another long drive ahead of me."

He put his hand on the door latch, paused with it there. "What'll you say to the man who hired you, the bail bondsman?"

193

What would I say to Abe Melikian? The truth — some of it, at least. Stephen Arthur Benson is dead and in the ground and what's left of his family is poor; the bail money's gone, Abe, and there's no way you can get any of it back; write it off your taxes and forget about it. He trusted me and my judgment and he wouldn't press for details, particularly not when I waived the balance of my fee.

"You let me worry about that," I said, and Benson shrugged and lifted himself out of the car. He seemed to want to say something else; instead he turned, walked to the store. There was nothing more to say. Neither thank-yous nor goodbyes were appropriate and we both knew it.

I watched him unlock the door, switch the window sign from *Closed* to *Open* before he disappeared into the dimness within. Then I drove out onto the highway and headed north. To San Francisco. To my office and my flat and Kerry.

Home is the place where.

Flood

She sat at the upstairs bedroom window, watching the river run wild below. Rain lay like crinkled cellophane wrap on the glass, so that everything outside seemed shimmery, distorted — the low-hanging, black-veined clouds, the half-submerged trees along the banks, the drift and wreckage riding the churning brown floodwaters. She could hear the sound of the water, a constant thrumming pulse, even with the rain beating a furious tattoo on the roof.

Nearly a week now of steady downpour, a chain of Pacific storms that had lashed northern California with winds up to a hundred miles per hour. It seemed to her that it had been raining much longer, that she could not remember a time when the sky was clear and blue and the sun shone. The rain was *inside* her, too. When she looked into the mirror, looked into her own eyes, what she saw was a wet, gray, swampy place, a sodden landscape like the one she watched through the window. One in which she was trapped, as she was physically trapped here and now. One from which there seemed to be no escape.

She shivered; it was cold in the room. They had been without heat or power for more than twenty-four hours. The fierce storm winds had toppled trees and power lines everywhere in the region. Roads were inundated and blocked by mudslides, one of them River Road fifty yards west of their house. Flood stage along these low-lying areas was thirty-two feet; the rising water had reached that mark

195

at eight last night, hours after the evacuation orders had been issued. It must be above forty feet now, at two in the afternoon. All the rooms downstairs were flooded halfway to their ceilings. The last time she'd looked, the car was totally covered and the only parts of the deck still visible were the tops of the support poles for the latticework roof. The roof itself had long since been torn off and carried away.

From the pocket of her pea jacket, as she had several times during the day, she took the ivory scrimshaw bowl. Smooth, round, heavy-bottomed, it fitted exactly the palm of her hand. Her grandfather had carved it from a walrus tusk and done the lacy scrimshawing in his spare time, during the period he'd worked as a mail carrier in Nome just after the Alaska Gold Rush. He'd given it to her mother, who in turn had passed it on to her only daughter. It had been the first thing she'd grabbed to bring upstairs with her when the in-pouring water forced them to abandon the lower floor. It was all she owned of any value, as Darrell so often reminded her.

"You and that damn bowl," he'd said this morning. "Well, you might as well hang onto it. We may need whatever we can sell it for someday. Nothing else of yours is worth half as much, God knows."

She stroked the cold surface, the intricate black pattern. It gave her comfort. Her only comfort in times of unhappiness and stress.

Shadows crawled thickly in the room — moist shadows laden with the brown-slime smell of the river. She found it difficult to breathe, but opening the window to let in fresh air would only worsen the stench. She thought of relighting one of the candles, to keep the shadows at bay, but the unsteady flame reflected off the window pane and made it even harder for her to see out. She was not sure why she wanted to keep looking out, but she did and she had all through the day. Compelled to sit here and watch the rain beat down, the murky, churning water rise higher and higher.

There would be another rescue boat along soon, maybe even one of the evacuation helicopters that were brought in when the floodwaters grew too dangerous for small craft. Rio Lomas, three miles to the east, had been cut off even longer than the River Road homes had, almost a day and a half; by now they would be airlifting evacuees to one of the larger towns inland, at a safe distance from the river. She wished that was where she was, in one of those towns, in an emergency shelter where she could be warm and dry, where the lights were bright and there was clean air to breathe.

Empty wish. Darrell wouldn't leave when the rescuers showed up. No matter how bad things were then, he wouldn't budge. He had refused evacuation in 1986, the worst flood in the river's history, when the waters crested at better than forty-eight feet. They had both come close to drowning that year, forced at the last to sit huddled in the attic crawlspace with the last dozen of his paintings wrapped in plastic sheeting like corpses awaiting burial. He'd refused to leave five years ago as well, the last time before this that the river had overrun its banks and made an island of their home. Stubborn. Fiercely possessive. Yes, and so many other less than endearing traits. So *many* others.

She rubbed the scrimshaw bowl and watched the rain slant down, the turmoil of conflicting currents and weird boils and eddy lines in the main channel, the soapy yellowish-white foam that scudded along what was left of the banks.

Why am I here? she thought.

I don't want to be here. I haven't wanted to be here in a long, long time.

The old, tired lament. And the old, tired response to it: I have nowhere else to go. Mom and Pop both gone, Jack blown up by a land mine in Vietnam, no other siblings or aunts or uncles or even a cousin. A few casual friends but none I can turn to, talk to, count on. Twenty-one years with Darrell, exactly half my life, and the twenty-one before him so far removed I can scarcely remember them. Where would I go? What could I do?

Sudden crashing noise from the far end of the house — Darrell's studio. He'd been drinking all day, and now he had reached the mean, tantrumy stage where he began breaking things. Splintering, tearing sounds reached her ears: he was at his paintings again. Not the better, finished ones. He never destroyed those oils and watercolors, no matter how drunk or frustrated or enraged he became, because they were his "true art" — the ones he believed were the work of an undiscovered, unappreciated genius; the ones he bitterly hoped to sell to summer tourists and the handful of local collectors, so they could pay their bills or at least keep their credit from being cut off altogether. No, his destructive wrath was reserved for the unfinished canvases, his "false starts," and for the unsold riverscapes and still-lifes and portraits of eccentric river dwellers that he'd decided were expendable, not quite up to his own lofty standards.

At first she, too, had believed he was a genius. A great and sensitive visionary. In those early days she had wanted to be an artist herself, at least an artisan. Not painting, nothing so important as that, just the designer and maker of earrings and pendants and other jewelry. She'd felt sure she had the talent to excel at this, but he had convinced her otherwise. Ridiculed and disparaged her efforts until, finally, she'd lost all enthusiasm and given up her work, her dreams, everything except her day-to-day existence as Mrs. Darrell

Boyd. But he'd succeeded not only in disillusioning her about her own abilities, but in giving her a true perspective on his as well. He was far less gifted than he considered himself to be, at best a shade or two above mediocre.

The description fit their marriage just as aptly. At best it had been a shade or two above mediocre. At worst —

Footsteps in the hallway, hard and lurching. She sat rigid, staring out through the rain-wavy glass. Waiting, steeling herself.

"Hey! Hey, you in there!"

She no longer had a name in her own house. She had become *Hey* or *Hey You* or harsh epithets just as impersonal.

"You hear me? I'm talking to you."

"I hear you, Darrell." Slowly she turned her head. He stood slouched in the doorway, shirt mostly unbuttoned and pulled free of his Levi's so that the bulge of his paunch showed. Unshaven, red-eyed, his graying hair a finger-rubbed tangle. She noticed all of that, and yet it was as though she were seeing him the way she had been seeing the storm-savaged river, through a pane of wavy glass. She looked away again before she said, "What do you want?"

"What d'you think I want?"

"I'm not a mind reader."

"What'd you do with it? Where'd you hide it this time?"

"Hide what?"

"You know what. Don't give me that."

"I don't touch your liquor. I never have."

"The hell you never have. There's another fifth, I brought it upstairs myself. What'd you do with it?"

"Look in the storeroom. That's where you put it."

"I know where *I* put it. Where'd *you* put it?"

"I never touched it, Darrell."

"Liar! Bitch!"

She didn't respond. Outside, something swirled past on the cocoa-brown water — a dead animal of some kind, a goat or large dog. She couldn't be sure because it was there one instant, bobbing and partly submerged, and the next it was gone.

"Where's that bottle, goddamn it? I'm warning you."

"In the storeroom," she said.

"That where you hid it?"

"It's been there all along."

"You go find it. Right now, you hear me?"

"I hear you."

"*Now*. Right this minute."

She got to her feet, not hurrying. Without looking at him she started across the room.

"And put that silly damn bowl away," he said. "Why d'you always have to keep playing with that thing, petting it like it's a fetish or something?"

She slipped the scrimshawed ivory back into her pocket, walked past him into the hallway. Each step was an effort, somehow, as if her legs — like the land, like the house itself — had become waterlogged.

The storeroom was between the bedroom and his studio. It had started out as her workspace, but when she'd given up jewelry-making it had gradually evolved into a catchall storage area. Boxes, oddments of furniture, unused canvases crowded it now, along with dust and spiderwebs. When they'd abandoned the lower floor this morning she had brought up as much food as they might need and whatever else could be salvaged, and put it in there. The perishables were on melting ice in the big cooler, the rest scattered on boxes and on the floor. She poked listlessly among the food

200

items and cartons, while he watched from the doorway. It took her less than a minute to find his last fifth of Scotch, more or less in plain sight behind the leg of a discarded table. She picked it up, held it out to him.

He snatched it from her hand. "Don't you ever do that again. Understand? You hide liquor from me again, you'll be sorry."

"All right," she said.

"Make me a sandwich," he said. "I'm hungry."

"What kind of sandwich?"

"What do I care what kind? A *sandwich*."

"All right."

"Make yourself useful for a change," he said, and stalked off with the bottle cradled like an infant against his chest.

She buttered bread, layered ham and processed cheese on top and then spread mustard on a second slice. Did it all mechanically, taking her time. She put the sandwich on a paper plate and brought it to the studio.

He was over by the tall double windows, squinting at one of his older riverscapes — trying to decide whether or not to destroy it, probably. He seemed even more misshapen and indistinct to her now, as if there was more than glass between them, as if she were looking at him underwater. She set the sandwich on his worktable, between the jars of oil paint and the now-open fifth of Scotch, and retreated to the hallway.

The open door to the bathroom drew her. She went inside and close to the medicine cabinet mirror, but it was too dark to make out her image clearly. She lit a candle and held it up. Her face, like his, seemed water-distorted, and when she peered at it from an inch or so away she could see the rain in her eyes. Behind her eyes. Rain and a turbulent, rising cataract like the one outside.

She snuffed the candle, returned to the bedroom and her

seat before the window. Rising, yes. The river's surface was a ferment spotted with debris — clumps of uprooted brush, logs and tree limbs bobbing drunkenly, a fence rail, the shattered remains of a rowboat, a child's red wagon. One of the logs slammed against the side wall of the house with enough force to crack boards, before it swirled away.

The rain continued to beat down in gray metallic sheets. The dark waters roared and shrieked like a wild creature caught in a snare, ripping at what was left of its banks, tearing them down and apart in a frenzy. She could *feel* the flood, cold, slimy on her face and the backs of her hands. Smell and taste it, too, rank and primitive.

And still the waters kept rising . . .

Abruptly she stood. On heavy legs, her mind blank, she went out and back to Darrell's studio. He was sitting hunched at the worktable, staring fixedly into tumbler of whiskey, the sandwich she'd made uneaten and pushed aside. His portable radio was on, tuned to a Santa Rosa station, the voice of a newscaster droning words that had no meaning for her. He did not hear her as she stepped up behind him; he had no idea she was there.

You've never known I was here, she thought. Just that one thought. Then her mind was blank again.

She took out the scrimshaw bowl, held it bottom side up in her hand. She no longer heard the newscast; she listened instead to the roaring and shrieking of the flood. Then, without hesitation, she raised the bowl and brought it down with all her strength on the back of his head.

He didn't make a sound. Or if he did, the raging of the waters drowned it out.

She had no difficulty dragging him across to the window. It was as if, dead or dying, he had become almost weightless. The wind flailed her with rain and surface spume as

202

she raised the sash, hoisted him onto the sill. The river was only a few feet below, all but filling the downstairs rooms; it boiled and frothed, creating little whirlpools clogged with flotsam. She pushed Darrell down into the brown turmoil. There was a splash, and two or three seconds later, no more than that, he wasn't there any more.

She was seated once again at the bedroom window when the rescue boat appeared. By then, mercifully, it had stopped raining and the floodwaters did not seem to be rising any longer. The worst was over. Everything was still gray and moist and chaotic, but there was a hint of clearing light in the grayness. She was sure of it — light outside and inside, both.

When she saw the boat rounding the bend she opened the window and waved her arms to show the rescuers where she was. They came straight to her at accelerated speed, two men wearing neoprene wetsuits hunched in the stern. She knew both of them; they were volunteer firemen in Rio Lomas.

As they drew alongside one of them called out, "Are you all right, Mrs. Boyd?"

She touched the freshly polished ivory bowl in her pocket. It was not the only thing of value she had; it never had been. "My name is Lee Anne," she said. "Lee Anne *Meeker*. Jewelry-maker."

"Are you all right?"

"Yes, I'm all right "

"Where's your husband?"

"Gone," she said.

"Gone? What do you mean, gone?"

She was not a liar; she told them the literal and absolute truth. "The flood took him," she said. "He was swept away in the flood."

A Cold Foggy Day

The two men stepped off the Boston-to-San Francisco plane at two o'clock on a cold foggy afternoon in February. The younger of the two by several years had sand-colored hair and a small birthmark on his right cheek; the older man had flat gray eyes and heavy black brows. Both wore topcoats and carried small overnight bags.

They walked through the terminal and down to one of the rental-car agencies on the lower level. The older man paid for the rental of a late-model sedan. When they stepped outside, the wind was blowing and the wall of fog eddied in gray waves across the airport complex. The younger man thrust his hands deep into the pockets of his topcoat as they crossed to the lot where the rental cars were kept. He could not remember when he had been quite so cold.

A boy in a white uniform brought their car around. The older man took the wheel. As he pulled the car out of the lot, the younger man said, "Turn the heater on, will you, Harry? I'm freezing in here."

Harry put on the heater. Warm air rushed against their feet, but it would be a long while before it was warm enough to suit the younger man. He sat blowing on his hands. "Is it always this cold out here?" he asked.

"It's not cold," Harry said.

"Well, I'm freezing."

"It's just the fog, Vince. You're not used to it."

"There's six inches of snow in Boston," Vince said. "Ice on the streets thick enough to skate on. But I'm damned if it's as cold as it is out here."

"You have to get used to it."

"I don't think I *could* get used to it," Vince said. "It cuts through you like a knife."

"The sun comes out around noon most days and burns off the fog," Harry said. "San Francisco has the mildest winters you've ever seen."

The younger man didn't say anything more. He didn't want to argue with Harry; this was Harry's home town. How could you argue with a man about his home town?

When they reached San Francisco, 20 minutes later, Harry drove a roundabout route to their hotel. It was an old but elegant place on Telegraph Hill, and the windows in their room had a panoramic view of the bay. Even with the fog, you could see the Golden Gate Bridge and the Bay Bridge and Alcatraz Island. Harry pointed out each of them.

But Vince was still cold and he said he wanted to take a hot shower. He stood under a steaming spray for ten minutes. When he came out again, Harry was still standing at the windows.

"Look at that view," Harry said, "Isn't that some view?"

"Sure," Vince agreed. "Some view."

"San Francisco is a beautiful city, Vince. It's the most beautiful city in the world."

"Then why did you ever leave it? Why did you come to Boston? You don't seem too happy there."

"Ambition," Harry said. "I had a chance to move up and I took it. But it's been a long time, Vince."

"You could always move back here."

"I'm going to do that," Harry said. "Now that I'm home again, I know I don't want to live anywhere else. I tell you, this is the most beautiful city anywhere on this earth."

Vince was silent. He wished Harry wouldn't keep talking about how beautiful San Francisco was. Vince liked Boston; it was his town just as San Francisco was Harry's. But Vince couldn't see talking about it all the time, the way Harry had ever since they'd left Boston this morning. Not that Vince would say anything about it. Harry had been around a long time and Vince was just a new man. He didn't know Harry that well — had only worked with him a few times; but everybody said you could learn a lot from him. And Vince wanted to learn.

That was not the only reason he wouldn't say anything about it. Vince knew why Harry was talking so much about San Francisco. It was to keep his mind off the job they had come here to do. Still, it probably wasn't doing him much good, or Vince any good either. The only way to take both their minds off the job was to get it done.

"When are we going after him, Harry?" Vince said.

"Tonight."

"Why not now?"

"Because I say so. We'll wait until tonight."

"Listen, Harry —"

"We're doing this my way, remember?" Harry said. "That was the agreement. *My* way."

"All right," Vince said, but he was beginning to feel more and more nervous about this whole thing with Dominic DiLucci. He wished it was over and finished with and he was back in Boston with his wife. Away from Harry.

After a while Harry suggested they go out to Fisherman's Wharf and get something to eat. Vince wasn't hungry and he didn't want to go to Fisherman's Wharf; all he wanted to do was to get the job over and done with. But Harry insisted, so he gave in. It was better to humor Harry than to complicate things by arguing with him.

They took a cable car to Fisherman's Wharf and walked around there for a time, in the fog and the chill wind. Vince was almost numb by the time Harry picked out a restaurant, but Harry didn't seem to be affected by the weather at all. He didn't even have his topcoat buttoned.

Harry sat by the window in the restaurant, not eating much, looking out at the fishing boats moored in the Wharf basin. He had his face close to the glass, like a kid.

Vince watched him and thought: he's stalling. Well, Vince could understand that, but understanding it didn't make it any easier. He said finally, "Harry, it's after seven. There's no sense in putting it off any longer."

Harry sighed. "I guess you're right."

"Sure I am."

"All right," Harry said.

He wanted to take the cable car back to their hotel, but Vince said it was too cold riding on one of those things. So they caught a taxi, and then picked up their rental car. Vince turned on the heater himself this time, as high as it would go.

Once they had turned out of the hotel garage, Vince said, "Where is he, Harry? You can tell me that now."

"Down the coast. Outside Pacifica."

"How far is that?"

"About twenty miles."

"Suppose he's not there?"

"He'll be there."

"I don't see how you can be so sure."

"He'll be there," Harry said.

"He could be in Mexico by now."

"He's not in Mexico," Harry said. "He's in a little cabin outside Pacifica."

Vince shrugged and decided not to press the point. This was Harry's show; he himself was along only as a back-up.

Harry drove them out to Golden Gate Park and through it and eventually onto the Coast Highway, identifying landmarks that were half hidden in fog. Vince didn't pay much attention; he was trying to forget his own nervousness by thinking about his wife back in Boston.

It took them almost an hour to get where they were going. Harry drove through Pacifica and beyond it several miles. Then he turned right, toward the ocean, onto a narrow dirt road that wound steadily upward through gnarled cypress and eucalyptus trees. That's what Harry said they were anyway. There was fog here too, thick and gray and roiling. Vince could almost feel the coldness of it, as if it were seeping into the car through the vents.

They passed several cabins, most of them dark, a couple with warm yellow light showing at the windows. Harry turned onto another road, pitted and dark, and after a few hundred yards they rounded a bend. Vince could see another cabin then. It was small and dark, perched on the edge of a cliff that fell away to the ocean. But the water was hidden by the thick fog.

Harry parked the car near the front door of the cabin. He shut off the engine and the headlights.

Vince said, "I don't see any lights."

"That doesn't mean anything."

"It doesn't look like he's here."

"He'll be here."

Vince didn't say anything. He didn't see how Harry could know with that much certainty that Dominic DiLucci was going to be here. You just didn't know anybody that well.

They left the warmth of the car. The wind was sharp and stinging, blowing across the top of the bluff from the sea. Vince shivered.

Harry knocked on the cabin door and they stood waiting. And after a few moments the door opened and a thin man with haunted eyes looked out. He was dressed in rumpled slacks and a white shirt that was soiled around the collar. He hadn't shaved in several days.

The man stood looking at Harry and didn't seem surprised to see him. At length he said, "Hello, Harry."

"Hello, Dom," Harry said.

They continued to look at each other. Dominic DiLucci said, "Well, it's cold out there." His voice was calm, controlled, but empty, as if there was no emotion left inside him. "Why don't you come in?"

They entered the cabin. A fire glowed on a brick hearth against one wall. Dom switched on a small lamp in the front room, and Vince saw that the furniture there was old and overstuffed, a man's furniture. He stood apart from the other two men, thinking that Harry had been right all along and that it wouldn't be long before the job was finished. But for some reason that didn't make him feel any less nervous. Or any less cold.

Harry said, "You don't seem surprised to see me, Dom."

"Surprised?" Dom said. "No, I'm not surprised. Nothing can surprise me any more."

"It's been a long time. You haven't changed much."

"Haven't I?" Dom said, and smiled a cold humorless smile.

"No," Harry said. "You came here. I knew you would. You always came here when you were troubled, when you wanted to get away from something."

Dominic DiLucci was silent.

Harry said, "Why did you do it, Dom?"

"Why? Because of Trudy, that's why."

"I don't follow that. I thought she'd left you, run off with somebody from Los Angeles."

"She did. But I love her, Harry, and I wanted her back. I thought I could buy her back with the money. I thought if I got in touch with her and told her I had a hundred thousand dollars, she'd come back and we could go off to Brazil or someplace."

"But she didn't come back, did she?"

"No. She called me a fool and a loser on the phone and hung up on me. I didn't know what to do then. The money didn't mean much without Trudy; nothing means much without her. Maybe I wanted to be caught after that, maybe that's why I stayed around here. And maybe you figured that out about me along with everything else."

"That's right," Harry said. "Trudy was right, too, you know. You *are* a fool and a loser, Dom."

"Is that all you have to say?"

"What do you want me to say?"

"Nothing, I guess. It's about what I expected from you. You have no feelings, Harry. There's nothing inside of you and there never was or will be."

Dom rubbed a hand across his face, and the hand was trembling. Harry just watched him. Vince watched him too, and he thought that Dominic DiLucci was about ready to crack; he was trying to bring it off as if he were in perfect control of himself, but he was ready to crack.

Vince said, "We'd better get going."

Dom glanced at him, the first time he had looked at him since they'd come inside. It didn't seem to matter to him who Vince was. "Yes," he said. "I suppose we'd better."

"Where's the money?" Harry asked him.

"In the bedroom. In a suitcase in the closet."

Vince went into the bedroom, found the suitcase, and looked inside. Then he closed it and came out into the front room again. Harry and Dom were no longer looking at each other.

They went outside and got into the rental car. Harry took the wheel again. Vince sat in the rear seat with Dominic DiLucci.

They drove back down to the Coast Highway and turned north toward San Francisco. They rode in silence. Vince was still cold, but he could feel perspiration under his arms. He glanced over at Dom beside him, sitting there with his hands trembling in his lap. From then on he kept his eyes on Harry.

When they came into San Francisco, Harry drove them up a winding avenue that led to the top of Twin Peaks. The fog had lifted somewhat, and from up there you could see the lights of the city strung out like misty beads along the bay.

As soon as the lights came into view Harry leaned forward, staring intently through the windshield. "Look at those lights," he said. "Magnificent. Isn't that the most magnificent sight you ever saw, Vince?"

And Vince understood then. All at once, in one stinging bite of perception, he understood the truth.

After Dominic DiLucci had stolen the $100,000 from the investment firm where he worked, Harry had told the San Francisco police that he didn't know where Dom could be. But then he had gone to the head of the big insurance company where he and Vince were both claims investigators — the same insurance company that handled the policy on Dom's investment firm — and had told the Chief that maybe he did have an idea where Dom was but hadn't said

211

anything to the police because he wanted to come out here himself, wanted to bring Dom in himself. Dom wasn't dangerous, he said; there wouldn't be any trouble.

The Chief hadn't liked the idea much, but he wanted the $100,000 recovered. So he had paid Harry's way to San Francisco, and Vince's way with him as a back-up man. Both Vince and the Chief had figured they knew why Harry wanted to come himself. But they had been wrong. Dead-wrong.

Harry DiLucci was still staring out at the lights of San Francisco. And he was smiling.

What kind of man are you? Vince thought. What kind of man sits there with his own brother in the back seat, on the way to jail and ready to crack — his own brother — and looks out at the lights of a city and smiles?

Vince shivered. This time it had nothing to do with the cold.

Engines

When Geena moved out and filed for divorce, the first two things I did were to put the house up for sale and to quit Unidyne, a job I'd hated from the beginning. Then I loaded the Jeep and drove straight to Death Valley.

I told no one where I was going. Not that there was anybody to tell, really; we had no close friends, or at least I didn't, and my folks were both dead. Geena could have guessed, of course. She knew me that well, though not nearly well enough to understand my motives.

I did not go to Death Valley because something in my life had died.

I went there to start living again.

October is one of the Valley's best months. All months in the Monument are good, as far as I'm concerned, even July and August, when the midday temperatures sometimes exceed 120 degrees Fahrenheit and Death Valley justifies its Paiute Indian name, *Tomesha* — ground afire. If a sere desert climate holds no terrors for you, if you respect it and accept it on its terms, survival is not a problem and the attractions far outweigh the drawbacks. Still, I'm partial to October, the early part of the month. The beginning of the tourist season is still a month away, temperatures seldom reach 100 degrees, and the constantly changing light show created by sun and wind and clouds is at its most spectacular. You can stay in one place all day, from dawn to dark — Zabriskie Point, say, or the sand dunes near Stovepipe Wells

213

— and with each ten-degree rise and fall of the sun the colors of rock and sand hills change from dark rose to burnished gold, from chocolate brown to purple and indigo and gray-black, with dozens of subtler shades in between.

It had been almost a year since I'd last been to the Valley. Much too long, but it had been a difficult year. I'd been alone on that last visit, as I was alone now; alone the last dozen or so trips, since Geena refused to come with me anymore five years ago. I preferred it that way. The Valley is a place to be shared only with someone who views it in the same perspective, not as endless miles of coarse, dead landscape but as a vast, almost mystical place — a *living* place — of majestic vistas and stark natural beauty.

Deciding where to go first hadn't been easy. It has more than three thousand square miles, second only among national parks to Yellowstone, and all sorts of terrain: the great trough of the valley floor, with its miles of salt pan two hundred feet and more below sea level, its dunes and alluvial fans, its borate deposits and old borax works, its barren fields of gravel and broken rock; and five enclosing mountain ranges full of hidden canyons, petroglyphs, played-out gold and silver mines, ghost towns. I'd spent an entire evening with my topos — topographical maps put out by the U.S. Geological Survey — and finally settled on the Funeral Mountains and the Chloride Cliffs topo. The Funerals form one of the eastern boundaries, and their foothills and crest not only are laden with a variety of canyons but contain the ruins of the Keane Wonder Mill and mine and the gold boomtown of Chloride City.

I left the Jeep north of Scotty's Castle, near Hells Gate, packed in, and stayed for three days and two nights. The first day was a little rough; even though I'm in good shape, it takes a while to refamiliarize yourself with desert mountain terrain after a year away. The second day was easier. I spent that one exploring Echo Canyon and then tramping among the thick-timbered tramways of the Keane, the decaying mill a mile below it which in the 1890s had twenty stamps processing eighteen hundred tons of ore a month. On the third day I went on up to the Funerals' sheer heights and Chloride City, and the climb neither strained nor winded me.

It was a fine three days. I saw no other people except at a long distance. I reestablished kinship with the Valley, as only a person who truly loves it can, and all the tension and restless dissatisfaction built up over the past year slowly bled out of me. I could literally feel my spirit reviving, starting to soar again.

I thought about Geena only once, on the morning of the third day as I stood atop one of the crags looking out toward Needles Eye. There was no wind, and the stillness, the utter absence of sound, was so acute it created an almost painful pressure against the eardrums. Of all the things Geena hated about Death Valley, its silence — "void of silence," an early explorer had termed it — topped the list. It terrified her. On our last trip together, when she'd caught me listening, she'd said, "What are you listening *to*? There's nothing to hear in this godforsaken place. It's as if everything has shut down. Not just here; everywhere. As if all the engines have quit working."

She was right, exactly right: as if all the engines have quit working. And that perception, more than anything else, summed up the differences between us. To her, the good things in life, the essence of life itself, were people, cities, constant scurrying activity. She needed to hear the steady, throbbing engines of civilization in order to feel safe, secure, alive. And I needed none of those things;

needed *not* to hear the engines.

I remembered something else she'd said to me once, not so long ago. "You're a dreamer, Scott, an unfocused dreamer. Drifting through life looking for something that might not even exist." Well, maybe there was truth in that too. But if I was looking for something, I had already found part of it right here in Death Valley. And now I could come here as often as I wanted, without restrictions; resigning from Unidyne had seen to that. I couldn't live in the Monument — permanent residence is limited to a small band of Paiutes and Park Service employees — but I could live nearby, in Beatty or Shoshone or one of the other little towns over in the Nevada desert. After the L.A. house sold, I'd be well fixed. And when the money finally did run out I could hire out as a guide, do odd jobs — whatever it took to support myself. Dreamer with a focus at last.

For a little time, thinking about Geena made me sad. But the Valley is not a place where I can feel sad for long. I had loved her very much at first, when we were both students at UCLA, but over our eleven years together the love had eroded and seeped away, and now what I felt mainly was relief. I was free and Geena was free. Endings don't have to be painful, not if you look at them as beginnings instead.

Late that third afternoon I hiked back to where I'd left the Jeep. No one had bothered it; I had never had any trouble with thieves or vandals out here. Before I crawled into my sleeping bag I sifted through the topos again to pick my next spot. I don't know why I chose the Manly Peak topo. Maybe because I hadn't been in the southern Panamints, through Warm Springs Canyon, in better than three years. Still, it was an odd choice to make. That region was not one of my favorite parts of the Valley. Also, a large portion of the area is under private claim, and the owners of the talc mines along the canyon take a dim view of trespassing; you have to be extra careful to keep to public lands when you pack in there.

In the morning, just before dawn, I ate a couple of nutrition bars for breakfast and then pointed the Jeep down Highway 178. The sun was out by the time I reached the Warm Springs Canyon turnoff. The main road in is unpaved, rutted and talc-covered, and primarily the domain of eighteen-wheelers passing to and from the mines. You need at least a four-wheel-drive vehicle to negotiate it and the even rougher trails that branch off it. I would not take a passenger car over one inch of that terrain. Neither would anyone else who knows the area or pays attention to the Park Service brochures, guidebooks, and posted signs.

That was why I was amazed when I came on the Ford Taurus.

I had turned off the main canyon road ten miles in, onto the trail into Butte Valley, and when I rounded a turn on the washboard surface there it was, pulled off into the shadow of a limestone shelf. The left rear tire was flat, and a stain that had spread out from underneath told me the oil pan was ruptured. No one was visible inside or anywhere in the immediate vicinity.

I brought the Jeep up behind and went to have a look. The Ford had been there awhile — that was clear. At least two days. The look and feel of the oil stain proved that. I had to be the first to come by since its abandonment, or it wouldn't still be sitting here like this. Not many hikers or offroaders venture out this way in the off-season, the big ore trucks use the main canyon road, and there aren't enough park rangers for daily backcountry patrols.

The Ford's side windows were so dust- and talc-caked that I could barely see through them. I tried the driver's door; it was unlocked. The interior was empty except for two things on the front seat. One was a woman's purse, open, the edge of a wallet poking out. The other was a piece of lined notepaper with writing on it in felt-tip pen, held down by the weight of the purse.

I slid the paper free. Date on top — two days ago — and below that, "To Frank Spicer," followed by several lines of shaky backhand printing. I sensed what it was even before I finished reading the words.

I have no hope left. You and Conners have seen to that. I can't fight you anymore and I can't go on not knowing if Kevin is safe, how you must be poisoning his mind even if you haven't hurt him physically. Someday he'll find out what kind of man you really are. Someday he *will* find out. And I pray to God he makes you pay for what you've done.

I love you, Kevin. God forgive me.

I couldn't quite decipher the scrawled signature. Christine or Christina something — not Spicer. I opened the wallet and fanned through the card section until I found her driver's license. The Ford had California plates, and the license had also been issued in this state. Christina Dunbar. Age 32. San Diego address. The face in the ID photo was slender and fair-haired and unsmiling.

The wallet contained one other photo, of a nice-looking boy eight or nine years old — a candid shot taken at a lake or large river. Kevin? Nothing else in the wallet told me anything. One credit card was all she owned. And twelve dollars in fives and singles.

I returned the wallet to the purse, folded the note in there with it. In my mouth was a dryness that had nothing to do with the day's gathering heat. And in my mind was a feeling of urgency much more intense than the situation called for. If she'd brought along a gun or pills or some other lethal device, she was long dead by now. If she'd wanted the Valley to do the job for her, plenty enough time had elapsed for that too, given the perilous terrain and the proliferation of sidewinders and daytime temperatures in the mid nineties and no water and improper clothing. Yet there was a chance she was still alive. A chance I could keep her that way if I could find her.

I tossed her purse into the Jeep, uncased my 7 x 50 Zeiss binoculars, and climbed up on the hood to scan the surrounding terrain. The valley floor here was flattish, mostly fields of fractured rock slashed by shallow washes. Clumps of low-growing creosote bush and turtleback were the only vegetation. I had a fairly good look over a radius of several hundred yards: no sign of her.

Some distance ahead there was higher ground. I drove too fast on the rough road, had to force myself to slow down. At the top of a rise I stopped again, climbed a jut of limestone to a notch in its crest. From there I had a much wider view, all the way to Striped Butte and the lower reaches of the Panamints.

The odds were against my spotting her, even with the powerful Zeiss glasses. The topography's rumpled irregularity created too many hidden places; she might have wandered miles in any direction. But I did locate her, and in less than ten minutes, and when I did I felt no surprise. It was as if, at some deep level, I'd been certain all along that I would.

She was a quarter of a mile away, to the southwest, at the bottom of a salt-streaked wash. Lying on her side, motionless, knees drawn up to her chest, face and part of her blond head hidden in the crook of one bare arm. It was impossible to tell at this distance if she was alive or dead.

The wash ran down out of the foothills like a long, twisted scar, close to the trail for some distance, then hooking away from it in a gradual snake-track curve. Where she lay was at least four hundred yards from the four-wheel track. I picked out a trail landmark roughly opposite, then scrambled back down to the Jeep.

It took me more than an hour to get to her: drive to the landmark, load my pack with two extra soft-plastic water bottles and the first-aid kit, strap the pack on, and then hike across humps and flats of broken rock as loose and treacherous as talus. Even though the prenoon temperature was still in the eighties, I was sweating heavily — and I'd used up a pint of water to replace the sweat loss — by the time I reached the wash.

She still lay in the same drawn-up position. And she didn't stir at the noises I made, the clatter of dislodged rocks, as I slid down the wash's bank. I went to one knee beside her, groped for a sunburned wrist. Pulse, faint and irregular. I did not realize until then that I had been holding my breath; I let it out thin and hissing between my teeth.

She wore only a thin, short-sleeved shirt, a pair of Levi's, and tattered Reeboks. The exposed areas of her skin were burned raw, coated with salt from dried sweat that was as gritty as fine sand; the top of her scalp was flecked with dried blood from ruptured blisters. I saw no snake or scorpion bites, no limb fractures or swellings. But she was badly dehydrated. At somewhere between 15 percent and 22 percent dehydration, a human being will die, and she was at or near the danger zone.

Gently I took hold of her shoulders, eased her over onto her back. Her limbs twitched; she made a little whimpering sound. She was on the edge of consciousness, more submerged than not. The sun's white glare hurt her eyes even through the tightly closed lids. She turned her head, lifted an arm painfully across the bridge of her nose.

I freed one of the foil-wrapped water bottles, slipped off the attached cap. Her lips were cracked, split deeply in a couple of places; I dribbled water on them, to get her to open them. Then I eased the spout into her mouth and squeezed out a few more drops.

At first she struggled, twisting her head, moaning deep in her throat: the part of her that wanted death rebelling against revival and awareness. But her will to live hadn't completely deserted her, and her thirst was too acute. She swallowed some of the warm liquid, swallowed more when I lifted her head and held it cushioned against my knee. Before long she was sucking greedily at the spout, like an infant at its mother's nipple. Her hands came up and clutched at the bottle; I let her take it away from me, let her drain it. The idea of parceling out water to a dehydration victim is a fallacy. You have to saturate the parched tissues as fast as possible to accelerate the restoration of normal functions.

I opened another bottle, raised her into a sitting position, and then gave it to her. Shelter was the next most important thing. I took the lightweight space blanket from my pack, unfolded it, and shook it out. A space blanket is five by seven feet, coated on one side with a filler of silver insulating material and reflective surface. Near where she lay, behind her to the east, I hand-scraped a sandy area free of rocks. Then I set up the blanket into a lean-to, using takedown tent poles to support the front edge and tying them off with nylon cord to rocks placed at a forty-five-degree angle from the shelter corners. I secured the ground side of the lean-to with more rocks and sand atop the blanket's edge.

Christina Dunbar was sitting slumped forward when I finished, her head cradled in her hands. The second water bottle, as empty as the first, lay beside her. I gripped her shoulders again, and this time she stiffened, fought me weakly as I drew her backward and pressed her down into the lean-to's shade. The struggles stopped when I pillowed her head with the pack. She lay still, half on her side, her eyes still squeezed tight shut. Conscious now but not ready to face either me or the fact that she was still alive.

The first-aid kit contained a tube of Neosporin. I said as I uncapped it, "I've got some burn medicine here. I'm going to rub it on your face and scalp first."

She made a throat sound that might have been a protest. But when I squeezed out some of the ointment and began to smooth it over her blistered skin, she remained passive. Lay there silent and rigid as I ministered to her.

I used the entire tube of Neosporin, most of it on her face and arms. None of the cuts and abrasions she'd suffered was serious; the medicine would disinfect those too. There was nothing I could do for the bruises on her upper arms, along her jaw, and on the left temple. I wondered where she'd got them. Not stumbling around in the desert: they were more than two days old, already fading.

When I was done I opened another quart of water, took a nutrition bar from my pack. Her eyes were open when I looked at her again. Gray-blue, dull with pain and exhaustion, staring fixedly at me without blinking. Hating me a little, I thought.

I said, "Take some more water," and extended the bottle to her.

"No."

"Still thirsty, aren't you?"

"No."

"We both know you are."

"Who're you?" Her voice was as dry and cracked as her lips, but strong enough. "How'd you find me?"

"Scott Davis. I was lucky. So are you."

"Lucky," she said.

"Drink the water, Christina."

"How do you know . . . ? Oh."

"That's right. I read the note."

"Why couldn't you just let me die? Why did you have to come along and find me?"

"Drink."

I held the bottle out close to her face. Her eyes shifted to it; the tip of her tongue flicked out, snakelike, as if she were tasting the water. Then, grimacing, she lifted onto an elbow and took the bottle with an angry, swiping gesture — anger directed at herself, not me, as if for an act of self-betrayal. She drank almost half of it, coughed and then lowered the bottle.

"Go a little slower with the rest of it."

"Leave me alone."

"I can't do that, Christina."

"I want to sleep."

"No, you don't." I unwrapped the nutrition bar. "Eat as much of this as you can get down. Slowly, little bites."

She shook her head, holding her arms stiff and tight against her sides.

"Please," I said.

"I don't want any food."

"Your body needs the nourishment."

"No."

"I'll force-feed you if I have to."

She held out a little longer, but her eyes were on the bar the entire time. When she finally took it, it was with the same gesture of self-loathing. Her first few bites were nibbles, but the honey taste revived her hunger, and she went at the bar the way she had at the water bottle. She almost choked on the first big chunk she tried to swallow. I made her slow down, sip water between each bite.

"How do you feel?" I asked when she was finished.

"Like I'm going to live, damn you."

"Good. We'll stay here for a while, until you're strong enough to walk."

"Walk where?"

"My Jeep, over on the trail. Four hundred yards or so, and the terrain is pretty rough. I don't want to have to carry you, at least not the whole way."

"Then what?"

"You need medical attention. There's an infirmary at Furnace Creek."

"And after that, the psycho ward," she said, but not as if she cared. "Where's the nearest one?"

I let that pass. "If you feel up to talking," I said, "I'm a good listener."

"About what?"

"Why you did this to yourself."

"Tried to kill myself, you mean. Commit suicide."

"All right. Why, Christina?"

"You read my note."

"It's pretty vague. Is Kevin your son?"

She winced when I spoke the name. Turned her head away without answering.

I didn't press it. Instead I shifted around and lay back on my elbows, with my upper body in the lean-to's shade. I was careful not to touch her. It was another windless day, and the near-noon stillness was as complete as it had been the other morning in the Funerals. For a time nothing moved anywhere; then a chuckwalla lizard scurried up the bank of the wash, followed a few seconds later by a horned toad. It looked as though the toad were chasing the lizard, but like so many things in the Valley, that was illusion. Toads and lizards are not enemies.

It was not long before Christina stirred and said, "Is there any more water?" Her tone had changed; there was resignation in it now, as if she had accepted, at least for the time being, the burden of remaining alive.

I sat up, took one of the last two full quarts from my pack. "Make this last until we're ready to leave," I said as I handed it to her. "It's a long walk to the Jeep, and we'll have to share the last bottle."

She nodded, drank less thirstily, and lowered the bottle with it still two-thirds full. That was a good sign. Her body was responding, its movements stronger and giving her less pain.

I let her have another energy bar. She took it without argument, ate it slowly with sips of water. Then she lifted herself into a sitting position, her head not quite touching the slant of the blanket. She was just a few inches over five feet, thin but wiry. The kind of body she had and the fact that she'd taken care of it was a major reason for her survival and swift recovery.

She said, "I guess you might as well know."

"If you want to tell me."

"Kevin's my son. Kevin Andrew Spicer. He'll be ten years old in December."

"Frank Spicer is your ex-husband?"

"Yes, and I hope his soul rots in hell."

"Custody battle?"

"Oh, yes, there was a custody battle. But I won. I had full legal custody of my son."

"Had?"

"Frank kidnapped him."

"You mean literally?"

"Literally."

"When?"

"A year and a half ago," Christina said. "He had visitation rights, every other weekend. He picked Kevin up one Friday afternoon and never brought him back. I haven't seen either of them since."

"The authorities couldn't find them?"

"Nobody could find them. Not the police, not the FBI, not any of the three private detectives I hired. I think they're still somewhere in the southwest — Nevada or Arizona or New Mexico. But I don't know. I don't know."

"How could they vanish so completely?"

"Money. Everything comes down to money."

"Not everything."

"He was a successful commercial artist. And bitter because he felt he was prostituting his great talent. Even after the settlement he had a net worth of more than two hundred thousand dollars."

"He liquidated all his assets before he took Kevin?"

"Every penny."

"He must've wanted the boy very badly."

"He did, but not because he loves him."

"To get back at you?"

"To hurt me. He hates me."

"Why? The custody battle?"

"That, and because I divorced him. He can't stand to lose any of his possessions."

"He sounds unstable."

"Unstable is a polite term for it. Frank Spicer is a para-
noid sociopath with delusions of grandeur. That's what a
psychiatrist I talked to called him."

"Abusive?"

"Not at first. Not until he started believing I was sleeping with everybody from the mayor to the mailman. I was
never unfaithful to him, not once."

"Did he abuse Kevin too?"

"No, thank God. He never touched Kevin. At least . . .
not before he took him away from me."

"You think he may have harmed the boy since?"

"He's capable of it. He's capable of anything. There's no
doubt of that now."

"Now?"

Headshake. She drank more water.

"Conners," I said. "Who's he?"

She winced again. "The last straw."

I waited, but she didn't go on. She was not ready to talk
about Conners yet.

"Christina, why did you come here?"

"I don't know. I was on the main road, and there was a
sign —"

"I mean Death Valley itself. All the way from San Diego,
nearly four hundred miles."

"I didn't drive here from San Diego."

"Isn't that where you live?"

"Yes, but I was in Las Vegas. I came from there."

"Why were you in Vegas?"

"Fool's errand," she said bitterly.

"Something happened there. What was it?"

She didn't answer. For more than a minute she sat stiffly,
squinting in the direction of Striped Butte; the sun, on its
anamorphic conglomeration of ribbons of crinoid lime-

stone, jasper, and mother minerals, was dazzling. Then —

"A man called me a few days ago. He said his name was Conners and he knew where Frank and Kevin were living, but he wanted a thousand dollars for the information. In cash, delivered to him in Vegas."

"Did you know him?"

"No."

"But you believed him."

"I wanted to believe him," she said. "He claimed to've known Frank years ago, to've had business dealings with him; he mentioned the names of people I knew. And the last detective I hired . . . he traced Frank and Kevin to a Vegas suburb six weeks ago. They disappeared again the day after he found out where they'd been staying."

"Why didn't you send the detective to meet with Conners?"

"He stopped working for me a month ago, when I couldn't pay him anymore. All the settlement money was gone, and I had nothing left to sell. And no friends left to borrow from."

"Then you couldn't raise the thousand Conners demanded?"

"No, I couldn't raise it. So I stole it."

I didn't say anything.

"I was desperate," she said. "Desperate and crazy."

"Where did you steal it?"

"From the hardware supply company where I work . . . worked. My boss is a nice guy. He loaned me money twice before, he was supportive and sympathetic, but he just couldn't loan me any more, he said. So I paid him back by taking a thousand dollars out of the company account. Easy; I was the office manager. Then I drove to Vegas and gave it to Conners."

"And it was all just a scam," I said. "He didn't know where Spicer and Kevin are."

"Oh, he knew, all right. He knew because Frank had set the whole thing up. That was part of the message Conners delivered afterward."

"Afterward?"

"After he beat me up and raped me."

"Jesus," I said.

"Frank is tired of being dogged by detectives. Frank says I'd better leave him and Kevin alone from now on. Frank says if I don't, there'll be more of the same, only next time he'll do it himself, and it won't just be rape and a beating — he'll kill me. End of message."

"Did you call the police?"

"What for? Conners isn't his real name, and he doesn't live in Vegas. What could the police have done except maybe arrest me and send me back to San Diego to stand trial for theft? No. No. I stayed in the motel room where it happened until I felt well enough to leave, and then I started driving. By the time the car quit on me I was way out here in the middle of nowhere and I didn't care anymore. I just didn't want to go on living."

"You still feel that way?"

"What do you think?"

I said, "There are a lot of miles between Vegas and Death Valley. And a lot of remote desert. Why did you come this far?"

"I don't know. I just kept driving, that's all."

"Have you ever been to the Valley before?"

"No."

"Was it on your mind? Death Valley, dead place, place to go and die?"

"No. I didn't even know where I was until I saw a sign.

What difference does it make?"

"It makes a difference. I think it does."

"Well, I don't. The only thing that matters is that you found me before it was too late."

She picked up the water bottle, sat holding it in brooding silence without drinking. I gave my attention to the Panamints, Manly Peak and the taller, hazy escarpments of Telescope Peak to the north. To some they were silent and brooding — bare monoliths of dark-gray basalt and limestone, like tombstones towering above a vast graveyard. But not to me. I saw them as old and benevolent guardians, comforting in their size and age and austerity. Nurturing. The Paiutes believe that little mountain spirits, *Kai-nu-suvs*, live deep in their rock recesses — kindly spirits, as beautiful as sunset clouds and as pure as fresh snow. When clouds mass above the peaks, the *Kai-nu-suvs* ride deer and bighorn sheep, driving their charges in wild rides among the crags. For such joyous celebrations of life, the Paiutes cherish them.

Time passed. I sat looking and listening. Mostly listening, until I grew aware of heat rays against my hands where they rested flat on my thighs. The sun had reached and passed its zenith, was robbing the shelter of its shade. If we didn't leave soon, I would have to reset the position of the lean-to.

"How do you feel?" I asked Christina. "Strong enough to try walking?"

She was still resigned. "I can try," she said.

"Stay where you are for a couple of minutes, while I get ready. I'll work around you."

I gathered and stowed the empty water bottles, took down the lean-to and stowed the stakes and then strapped on the pack. When I helped Christina to her feet she seemed able to stand all right without leaning on me. I shook out the blanket, draped it over her head and shoulders so that her arms were covered, showed her how to hold it in place under her chin. Then I slipped an arm around her thin body and we set out.

It was a long, slow trek to the Jeep. And a painful one for her, though she didn't complain, didn't speak the entire time. We stayed in the wash most of the way, despite the fact that it added a third as much distance, because the footing was easier for her. I stopped frequently so she could rest; and I let her have almost all the remaining water. Still, by the time we reached the trail her legs were wobbly and most of her new-gained strength was gone. I had to swing her up and carry her the last two hundred yards. But it was not much of a strain. She was like a child in my arms.

I eased her into the passenger seat, took the blanket, and put it and my pack into the rear. There were two quarts of water left back there. I drank from one, two long swallows, before I slid in under the wheel. She had slumped down limply in the other seat, with her head back and her eyes shut. Her breath came and went in ragged little pants.

"Christina?"

"I'm awake," she said.

"Here. More water."

She drank without opening her eyes.

I said, "There are some things I want to say before we go. Something important that needs to be settled."

"What would that be?"

"When we get to Furnace Creek, I'm not going to report you as an attempted suicide. We'll say you made the mistake of driving out here in a passenger car, and when it broke down you tried to walk out and lost your sense of direction. That sort of thing happens a dozen times a year in the

Valley. The rangers won't think anything of it."

"Why bother? It doesn't matter if you report me as a psycho case."

"You're not a psycho case. And it does matter. I want to keep on helping you."

"There's nothing you can do for me."

"I can help you find your son."

Her head jerked up; she opened her eyes to stare at me. "What're you talking about?"

"Just what I said. I want to help you find your son and take him back from his father."

"You can't be serious."

"I've never been more serious."

"But why would you . . . ?"

"A lot of reasons. Because you're still alive and I'd like you to stay that way. Because I don't want Frank Spicer to get away with kidnapping Kevin or with having you raped and beaten. Because it's right. Because I can."

She shook her head: trying to shake away disbelief so she could cling to hope again. "The heat must have made you crazy. I told you, I'm a fugitive; I stole money from my boss in San Diego —"

"You also told me he was supportive and sympathetic. Chances are he still is, or will be if he gets his thousand dollars back. I'll call him tonight, explain the situation, offer to send him the money right away if he drops any charges he may have filed. With interest, if he asks for it."

"My God, you'd do that?"

"You can pay me back after we find Kevin. Money's not a problem, Christina. I have more than enough for both of us."

"But Frank . . . you don't know him. He meant what he said about killing me. He'd kill you too."

"He won't harm either of us, I'll see to that. Or Kevin, if I can help it. I'm not afraid of men like Frank Spicer. He may be disturbed, but he's also a coward. Sending Conners proves that."

Another headshake. "How could we hope to find them? The FBI couldn't in a year and a half, the detectives couldn't. . . ."

"They didn't spend all their time looking," I said. "You and I can, as long as it takes. Time's not a problem, either. Before I came out here my wife filed for divorce and I quit my job. That part of my life is over. There's nothing to keep me from spending the rest of it any way I see fit."

"Why *this* way? Why would you do so much for a stranger? What do you expect to get out of it?"

"Nothing from you, Christina. It's as much for myself as it is for you."

"I want to believe you, but I just . . . I don't understand. Are you trying to be some kind of hero?"

"There's nothing heroic about me. My wife once called me an unfocused dreamer, drifting through life looking for something that might not even exist. She was half right. What I've been looking for I've had all along without realizing it — Death Valley, and my relationship to it. I've been coming here ever since I was a kid, more than twenty years, and I've always felt that it's a living place, not a dead one. Now . . . it seems almost sentient to me. As if it were responsible for bringing us together. I could have gone anywhere in three thousand square miles today, and I came to the exact spot you did two days ago; I could easily have missed finding you, but I didn't. The feeling of sentience is illusion, I suppose, but that doesn't make it any less important. If I don't finish saving your life — help you find your son, give you a reason to go on living — then none of what's

233

happened today will mean anything. And my relationship with the Valley will never be the same again. Does that make any sense to you?"

"Maybe," she said slowly. "Maybe it does."

"Will you let me finish what's been started, then? For your son's sake, if not for yours or mine?"

She had no words yet. Her head turned away from me, and at first I thought she was staring out through the windshield. Then some of the hurt smoothed out of her ravaged face, and her expression grew almost rapt, and I knew she wasn't looking at anything. Knew, too, what her answer would be. And that there was a closer bond between us than I'd thought.

She was listening.

What are you listening to? *There's nothing to hear in this godforsaken place.*

Yes, there was. Geena just hadn't been able to hear it.

It's as if everything has shut down. Not just here; everywhere. As if all the engines have quit working.

No, not all. There was still one engine you could hear if you tried hard enough. The engine I'd been listening to out in the wash, when I'd been making up my mind about Christina and Kevin and Frank Spicer. The engine she was listening to now. One engine clear and steady in the void of silence, the only one that really counts.

Your own.